"Stay with Me Tonight, Sabina."

She felt the rush of desire envelop her, and then the worry. "Are you sure you're not confusing your emotions, Miguel?"

"I have wanted you since I saw you ride that first race at San Felipe. You were magnificent."

"I came in last!"

"It was amazing that nag even made it around the track. But you rode beautifully." He ran his hands through her hair. "It was seeing you that made me realize it was all over with Natasha. I couldn't love her and feel that way about you. No woman had ever made me feel that way before. I love you, Sabina."

Dear Reader:

There is an electricity between two people in love that makes everything they do magic, larger than life. This is what we bring you in SILHOUETTE INTIMATE MOMENTS.

SILHOUETTE INTIMATE MOMENTS are longer, more sensuous romance novels filled with adventure, suspense, glamor or melodrama. These books have an element no one else has tapped: excitement.

We are proud to present the very best romance has to offer from the very best romance writers. In the coming months look for some of your favorite authors such as Elizabeth Lowell, Nora Roberts, Erin St. Claire and Brooke Hastings.

SILHOUETTE INTIMATE MOMENTS are for the woman who wants more than she has ever had before. These books are for you.

Karen Solem
Editor-in-Chief
Silhouette Books

Race Against The Wind

Sue Ellen Cole

Silhouette Intimate Moments
Published by Silhouette Books New York

America's Publisher of Contemporary Romance

Other Silhouette Books by Sue Ellen Cole

A Distant Castle

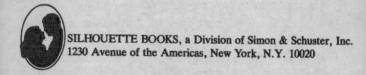

SILHOUETTE BOOKS, a Division of Simon & Schuster, Inc.
1230 Avenue of the Americas, New York, N.Y. 10020

ISBN: 0-671-46042-0

First Silhouette Books printing December, 1983

10 9 8 7 6 5 4 3 2 1

America's Publisher of Contemporary Romance

Printed in the U.S.A.

Horses surprise you all the time. You think you know what's going to happen. But in a big race, the best horses find a way to win.

—Laffit Pincay

Los Angeles Times, April 3, 1983

A special thanks to Kristyn Goddard, president of The Women's Jockey Association of Tarzana, California, for inviting me to the fascinating seminars and allowing me to observe the jockey classes.

I saw enough guts, determination and unbridled enthusiasm in that class of young women to put a battalion of bullfighters to shame.

And I am much indebted to jockey Denice Dietrick who took me behind the scenes, introducing me to jockeys, trainers and a host of wonderfully helpful people. Without her generosity and insights *Race Against the Wind* could not have been written.

Race Against The Wind

Chapter 1

SABINA BUCKLED HER CHIN STRAP, THEN TOOK THE reins while trainer Frank Lathrop gave her a leg up onto the nervous thoroughbred.

"Let someone else set the pace for the first quarter," Frank told her, "then let him out."

"Easy for you to say," she joked as she tied the knot in the reins. The three-year-old colt was going to be a handful. He was a sprinter rather than a long distance runner, and it would be all she could do to hold him back and conserve his strength for the final stretch.

Frank flashed her a confident smile for the benefit of the owner, a leathery, face-lifted actor who had bought the expensive four-legged toy as a glamorous tax shelter. As much as he professed a desire to see Gusty Guy in the winners' circle, Sabina knew as well as Frank that if the horse ever began to win with any consistency, the actor would dump him faster than he'd dumped any of his previous four wives.

Gusty Guy, an unlikely prospect to fatten any bank account with his winnings, was guaranteed to keep the IRS at bay. Even the bettors were only giving him 60–1 odds. Sabina would be lucky to get him to place. But there was always the chance. Gusty was a willing horse, and had been performing better and better with each race.

She glanced at her competition in the walking ring. It was breathtaking to realize that she was among some of the finest jockeys, thoroughbreds and trainers in the world. Not for the first time in the last few months, she resisted the temptation to pinch herself. If this was a dream, she wasn't going to risk waking up and spoiling it.

Other women jockeys she knew thought she had been crazy to come to San Felipe Meadows. "They'll never put you on anything but longshots," warned a friend, "if you get to race at all. The San Felipe trainers have barely made the miraculous discovery that women can exercise and groom horses. Tell 'em you're a jockey, and they'll laugh you off the track."

With over two thousand wins behind her, Sabina was hardly a novice rider, but she had ridden in the Midwest, the so-called bush leagues, where women jockeys were no longer such a novelty. But money, prestige and the best horses were in Southern California. And this was a make it or break it year. She was twenty-six, and despite race track legends like Johnny Longden, who had ridden winners until he was fifty-nine, jockeys had the dubious longevity of athletes in any sport. An older rider might have superior skill and experience, but he was no match against the strength and stamina of youth.

A legend in his own right, with over five thousand wins at the age of thirty-eight, Miguel Carrasco was mounting the horse beside her. Sabina watched him knot the reins. There was style in everything he did. If she had gained nothing else from these few months at San Felipe, it had been worth every moment just to observe Carrasco.

On his own two feet, he moved with the well-tuned, sinewy grace of a thoroughbred; and in the saddle it was as though the two athletes, one equine, the other human, were of one body. She had once seen a slow motion film of Carrasco riding, and the beautiful synchronous rhythm, the ripple of muscles beneath the silks, gave her sensations that were alarmingly erotic.

She wasn't the only woman he affected that way. His roguish smile, heavy-lidded dark eyes, and taut, rugged features attracted feminine attention wherever he went. As they paraded to post through the tunnel, the "jockey chasers" or track groupies, squealed and called out his name.

But that would be as close as any of them actually came to Miguel Carrasco. With a yearly salary in the millions, he belonged to the social set that viewed his races from the exclusive San Felipe Turf Club. He golfed with ex-presidents in Palm Springs and sailed with nobility on the French Riviera. He had been linked with many extraordinary and beautiful women, most recently, Natasha Ivanov, prima ballerina of the Los Angeles Ballet.

It was the last race of the afternoon. The

Southern California sun was slanting golden rays onto the track while the majestic San Felipe mountains were turning lavender blue with the dusk. The tall, slender palm trees, a trademark of the racetrack, reached skyward in graceful black silhouettes against the mountains.

It was a Saturday, and the stands that had been filled to capacity were now beginning to empty as the bettors ran their own race to the parking lots to beat the rush.

Sabina liked the elegant look of San Felipe Meadows, with its trim green lawns and carefully tended flower beds. It was a welcome change from the seedy fair ground tracks of the last few years.

As they paraded past the stands a slight breeze blew a pari-mutuel ticket onto the track. Miguel's horse leaped to one side, snorting in terror.

"Easy, now," she heard Miguel say as he calmed Composure, an ill-named brute of a horse. The only thing in his favor was speed. He had been clocked as one of the fastest three-year-olds at San Felipe that year, a potential for Kentucky—if he could keep a rider on his back long enough to make it to the finish line.

Had he been born human, Composure would probably have been a hatchet murderer. Not many jockeys cared to tangle with him. Thrashing around in his chute at the starting gate a few weeks before, he had landed his jockey in the hospital with multiple back injuries. Miguel Carrasco did not look concerned. He had a reputation for taking juvenile delinquent colts and turning them into Eagle Scouts. But despite his skill, he was having trouble maneuvering Composure into the starting gate. No doubt the horse was recalling his last unpleasant experience there. Sabina, in the next chute, was watching him cajole the feisty horse, who kicked and bit at the assistant starter. Miguel continued urging the colt forward with his hands and talking in a low voice.

If that was the tone he used to seduce women, he would never have to sleep alone, thought Sabina. The horse finally complied, but she could see that he was far from happy to be there. She held her breath and prayed the flag would go up soon so that Miguel could get out onto the track, where the chance of dangerous injury was slightly less.

Miguel continued talking quietly to the animal, and the colt finally stopped pawing the ground. He pricked up his ears as though considering Miguel's suggestions about his behavior.

"You're a magician," she said to Miguel.

"A horse psychiatrist is more like it," he said with a laugh, then looked at Sabina with concern. "Hey, pretty one, put your goggles down."

She had been so preoccupied with Composure, she had forgotten that essential step. It would make a difference when she was flying down the track at thirty-five miles an hour with hooves kicking up hard clods of dirt in her face. In fact, without protective goggles, she would have been forced to run ten lengths behind the rest or risk going blind.

Sabina smiled at him. "Thanks."

She still had to get used to the gallantry at San Felipe. On the rough fair-ground circuit, it was every jockey for himself. If your goggles weren't down, especially if you were on a favorite, nobody brought it to your attention. And dirty tricks were the rule rather than the exception. Once, when she was coming up alongside another rider, he reached over with his whip and brought it down on her back.

But here she had once been surprised to see a jockey move aside when she was on a faster horse and needed room to pass. At first she thought they were being kind because she was a woman; then she noticed that the male jockeys extended the same consideration to each other. At San Felipe, one jockey could beat out another in a $100,000 stakes race and go out to dinner with him that same night. At the racetracks she'd known, they would have been at each other's throats. This was a gentleman's club.

The flag was up. The gates clanged open. Sabina felt a surge of adrenaline as the seven powerful horses thundered onto the track. Her arm muscles grew taut; her legs locked into place; her wits sharpened.

Miguel Carrasco was to her left on the rail. Suddenly his horse bolted, hitting her and knocking her to the outside.

Gusty crossed his legs. She felt herself going over and struggled to stay in the saddle. With the other horses following, she would be trampled as soon as she hit the dirt.

It wouldn't be the first time. Knowing how that felt, she threw all her concentration into getting Gusty straightened out under her.

Miguel's horse, in a panic, plunged wildly into the heels of the horse in front of him. Composure went down, and Miguel was flung hard against the rail.

Sabina froze. The sight of Miguel sprawled on the ground paralyzed her with terror, that reached far beyond her own danger.

She was no longer at San Felipe, but back in Colorado. And it was not Miguel crumpled up on the ground, but Al.

No, Sabina, fight against the fear. Fight it, or you'll be down there yourself. Relax.

Movement returned to her fingers, and with it, contact with the horse's sensitive mouth. He was straightening out under her, still tense, but moving ahead.

Out of the corner of her eye she saw the medics rushing toward Miguel Carrasco from the infield.

Don't look back. Think about the race. There's nothing you can do for him. Nothing you could have done for Al.

Gusty was still tense from the trauma, bowing his neck, fighting against the bit.

"Relax, Gusty," she told him. "We've still got some track left."

Sabina's arms were aching now with the strain of holding him in. Then she saw a hole open up in the group of horses in front of her and decided to take the chance.

Anxious to run, Gusty stretched out his neck and easily moved through the others. They were now laying third. With a little more power Gusty had a good chance to make it.

There was no reason to go to the whip. She could feel the colt reaching, giving everything he had. Besides, she knew from having raced him before that he didn't respond to a heavy hand.

He was gaining on jockey Paul McDonald's horse, which had been favored to win. With the natural racing instinct that was bred into every thoroughbred, Gusty pushed ahead. They were edging forward, a length behind the lead. She chirped to him, and he moved by McDonald.

Then, as they came up to the eighth pole, where the starting gate had been positioned, Gusty saw the marks the gate had left in the ground and, without warning, hurdled them. Sabina had shown jumping horses as a teenager, and fortunately the action was reflex for her. She went with the rolling motion, but the hurdling made Gusty lose ground. In seconds Paul McDonald's horse came up from behind and passed her as they neared the sixteenth pole. Sabina tried to make up the ground, but Gusty had lost his edge and was tiring.

As she pulled the horse up in fourth place, she patted Gusty on the neck. "What the heck, pal, you tried. Next time I'll get him to put blinkers on you, and we'll win it."

After she had dismounted, Frank was waiting for her at the tunnel with the owner. "What the hell happened out there?" he asked angrily. She gave him a confused look. What could he possibly be angry about? Gusty had just run the race of his life.

Before she could answer, he continued, bristling with irritation. "I told you to rate him. You had no business wasting him at the beginning. Why didn't you use the whip on him in the stretch?"

Suddenly she understood. It was just another one of Frank's post-race tirades. This was part of the game Frank played with owners because he thought it impressed them. Usually she kept her mouth shut, but today she thought that both she and the colt had done remarkably well, and the owner should know about it.

"Gusty was shaken when Carrasco's horse went down. You probably didn't see it from where you were, but we were bumped pretty bad. Still, Gusty rallied, and we would probably have placed second if he hadn't hurdled the gate tracks."

"The gate tracks? Why the hell did you let him do something dumb like that?"

Before, she had been miffed. Now she was angry. Frank knew there was no way she could have prevented that. But the owner didn't. "You know damn well that horse jumps at his own shadow. If you had any sense, you would have run him with blinkers like I suggested last week."

Frank's face turned a blustery red. It was too late to take her words back. Frank Lathrop was the only trainer at San Felipe who was letting her race. By arguing with him, she was taking a chance he'd take her off his horses. But she was fed up with his bullying.

"If you don't like the way I train, maybe you ought to find someone else's horses to ride," he yelled after her as she walked into the jockey room.

"That idiot hassling you again?" asked Paul McDonald as she walked through the door.

"What else is new?" She pulled off her helmet.

"Don't take it personally. Lathrop likes to hear himself yell. He yells at everyone. Just ignore him. He knows damn well you were getting a lot out of that horse."

She shrugged. "My talking back probably wasn't the smartest thing, but what's done is done. Have you heard anything about Miguel?"

"He got up, but he was limping, so they hauled him off to the hospital for X-rays."

"I hope he's all right."

"Carrasco?" he said with a laugh that she could see masked his own concern. "He's made of reinforced concrete."

"Well, if you see him, give him my regards," she said, and slipped behind the partition that had been set up for her.

Whenever there was an accident, even at a racetrack as far away as New York, it dominated the conversation in the jockey's room. Everyone had suffered spills and identified with the pain. That it was Miguel, a close friend, made the empathy that much more intense.

"What happened to that S.O.B., Composure?" asked one of the jockeys.

"Pulled up lame. He's getting X-rays too."

"He may be a speed horse, all right, but you can't tell what the hell he's going to do. I won't ride him."

"They ought to retire him to stud. That's about all I can see he's good for."

"Or convert him to dog food."

They all laughed.

Outside the jockey's room Bardy Mulligan, one of the trainers, was talking about Miguel. Sabina stopped to listen.

"They want to keep him overnight at the hospital."

"He's going to love that." Paul chuckled. "We all ought to go over there tonight to cheer him up."

Sabina listened to them make plans. She would have liked to have gone. Miguel Carrasco had been friendly and helpful, even complimenting her riding, from the first day she'd begun riding at San Felipe.

It wasn't as though an engraved invitation were necessary to visit someone in a hospital, but she would feel awkward about just showing up. She still felt somewhat an outsider to their tightly knit circle.

As the group started to break up, Paul turned toward her. "You'll meet us there, won't you? I know Miguel's very fond of you. Seeing you would sure cheer him up."

As soon as Paul said that Miguel was fond of her, Sabina felt a warmth around her chest.

Although several of the jockeys had asked her out, Miguel never had. They had carried on some harmless flirting in the jockey's room, but she didn't really think he was interested in becoming anything more than a friend.

Rumor had it that he was very involved with the ballerina. And she would not have gone out with him anyway. It was still too soon after Al's death to do any dating. And when she was ready for a new relationship, she vowed it wouldn't be with another jockey. It was one thing to put one's own life on the line out there without worrying about the man you loved. The injuries he sustained could be more painful for a woman than her own.

After watching Miguel being flung against the rail today, she wondered if the scars left by Al's death would ever completely heal.

"Which hospital?" she asked Paul.

"Saint Joseph's. But listen, if you want, Janice and I could pick you up at your apartment."

"That would be wonderful. I have no idea where the hospital is, and I have absolutely no sense of direction."

"Hey, that's not true. I saw the way you maneuvered that horse around the track this afternoon. You've got a hell of a sense of direc-tion."

Sabina couldn't help thinking that being includ-ed was due in some measure to the way she had run the last race. That realization helped mitigate some of the bitterness of Frank's remarks.

Now that she'd had a chance to cool off, she was fully aware that Frank Lathrop was still her only ticket to the starting gate. She'd be a fool to let it go, when all it would probably cost her was an apology. Sabina started to walk back to Frank's barn to try to make amends.

No, her first instinct had been correct. Racing was her life, but self-respect was more important. She had done well with his horses. If he appreciat-ed it, he would keep her on them. If not, she'd go barn to barn and try to scare up another mount.

It wasn't likely her agent would do much to help her. On arriving at San Felipe, she had approached several agents without luck. This one had taken her book reluctantly even after review-ing her impressive winning record.

"I don't know a single trainer at San Felipe who's ever hired a girl jockey," he had said.

"You'd probably do better in the Bay area if you're set on riding in California. Things are a little looser up there."

She had gotten Frank's horses by approaching him directly at the track, and though her agent had taken his twenty-five percent just the same, he had still not managed to find her other trainer's horses to ride.

When Sabina had first moved back to California, she'd considered moving in with her parents. They were only twenty minutes away from the track by freeway, but she had been on her own too long, and though she didn't have much money, she preferred to rent a small studio apartment close to the track in San Felipe.

She didn't require much space; years of living in motel rooms, following the fair ground circuit, had given her Spartan tastes. With the exception of a comfortable blue armchair she'd found at a garage sale, she had left the furnished apartment intact, and made the dreary place her own by plastering the walls with race track photos and memorabilia.

Checking the messages on her phone answering machine, she learned that her agent had called. Hoping for the best, she rang him back.

"What happened out there today?" he asked abruptly.

"I came in fourth on Gusty Guy. He was a sixty to one . . ."

"Not in the race," he interrupted her. "I mean afterward. Frank Lathrop just called and canceled all your mounts."

She rubbed her tense neck muscles. "We had a

slight disagreement. Can you get me anything else next week?"

"I'll try," he said unenthusiastically. "But you know how it is."

"Yes, I know. But it's not as if I'm unknown out there anymore. I've done a good job on Lathrop's horses, which are no great shakes. I'm sure if you tried . . ."

"Look, honey, you can't go out there and get in knock-down drag outs with these guys. It's hard enough to get 'em to consider a girl jock. You get a reputation for being a prima donna, and I won't be able to get you a tricycle to ride."

She took a deep breath so that she wouldn't fly off the handle and tell him he hadn't even managed to get her a tricycle yet. Now that she'd lost Lathrop, she needed all the good will she could get. "Well, give it a try. I'll make the rounds of the barns again tomorrow morning."

"I hate to be pessimistic, but I think that's your best bet. And I know you're against that kind of thing, but you're a good-looking gal, Sabina. It wouldn't hurt you to go out with some of those guys."

"Thanks for the advice, but I'll go back to mucking stalls before I get a horse that way."

She stepped into the shower and let the hot water run onto her for a long time, trying to wash off the day's disappointments. Shampooing her hair made her feel slightly better. For racing, she wore her long, thick chestnut hair in a long braid down her back, to keep it out of her eyes. Now she set it in rollers and settled herself under the hairdryer.

At least she was going somewhere tonight,

even if it was just to a hospital. Sitting at home considering her future prospects at San Felipe could be depressing.

She took some time with her makeup and clothes that night. The people who would be there had only seen her in jeans or racing silks. It would be a shock for them to learn that she owned dresses like other women. Donning a softly clinging pale-rose dress that highlighted her olive skin tone, she let her long, slightly curled chestnut hair drape over her shoulders.

Paul and Janice MacDonald picked her up shortly before seven. "Bardy called just before we left," Paul told her. "Miguel's already checked himself out of the hospital."

"He hates hospitals," added Janice.

In the past two months she had met a few of the jockey's wives. Janice MacDonald, a world-class show rider, was one of the few who did not feel threatened by Sabina's close proximity to her husband during the various stages of undress in the jockey room.

"Have you ever been to Miguel's house before?" Janice asked her.

"Never."

"Then you're in for an experience." Janice's eyes twinkled.

"Why did the doctors want to keep him overnight?" asked Sabina. "Was he hurt so badly?"

"Not from this afternoon's spill," said Paul, "but they might have wanted to check out some old injuries. Like all of us, he's taken a few good falls in his time. Couple of years ago he broke his femur bone and was out for a year."

"Doctors thought he should retire from racing," said Janice, "but he ignored them and made a spectacular comeback, winning six races in one day."

The two-story, English Tudor–style home was located in an exclusive area of San Felipe, set on two acres of rolling lawns and shade trees. A maid greeted them at the door.

"Everyone is upstairs in Mr. Carrasco's bedroom," she said, and after taking their coats, led the way through the entry hall.

"I see what you mean," Sabina whispered to Janice as she glanced down at the inlaid parquet floor of the entry hall and up at the high wood-beamed ceiling. The graceful staircase with polished carved oak banisters was covered with plush forest green carpet.

On the walls were expensively framed paintings and lithographs of hunting and racing scenes. The color scheme of the entire house seemed to have been borrowed from the art work, with accents of forest green and burgundy.

Perhaps because a jockey's life was a hard one, few of them hailed from the moneyed or priveleged classes. But from what Sabina saw around her, she suspected Carrasco was not the typical jockey. His home looked like the ancestral estate of a man born into landed aristocracy, to whom wealth and privilege were nothing novel.

The uproarious laughter coming from the room at the end of the long hallway told them where Miguel's bedroom was before the maid could direct them there.

The spacious room was carpeted in light gray. Against one wall was a large brick fireplace where a cheerful fire burned. Across one entire wall were floor to ceiling French windows, and in the corner was a servant mixing drinks at a bar. There was still plenty of space left over for a couch and chairs, upholstered in burgundy corduroy.

If it weren't for the huge brass bed with the burgundy velvet bedspread at the far end of the room, it would seem more like a living room than a bedroom. "I can see why he preferred this to a hospital room," she whispered to Janice.

"Wouldn't you?"

"I'd prefer it to almost anything."

"You're probably not the first woman who's walked in here and said that."

Miguel was on the bed, propped up against a profusion of pillows, wearing a Japanese–style robe of a geometric black-and-white design. Sabina immediately found herself wondering if he were naked under it. Tied at the waist, the robe left his strongly muscled chest tantalizingly bare.

Sabina had always thought him a sexy man. There had been many times in the last few months when she'd seen him draped only in a towel in the jockey room and had marveled at the man's muscles. Seeing him like this, stretched out sensuously lynxlike on the burgundy bed, however, jammed her senses into high gear.

"Hola!" he called out to them and motioned them over.

There was a gargantuan flower arrangement on his bedstand studded with pari-mutuel tickets.

Janice leaned over the bed and kissed him on the cheek. "I thought you promised me never to fall off one of those dumb animals again. How are you feeling?"

"Lousy, but doped up with pain killers for the moment." He turned toward Sabina, looked her up and down, and grinned. "But what lovely consolation you've brought to relieve my misery."

He took Sabina's hand and pulled her down onto the bed beside him. "How beautiful you look with your hair like this." He touched her hair and let some of the silky strands slip through his fingers. "I hardly recognize you without your helmet."

There was a glow in his dark, sultry eyes that was making her feel giddy. It was tempting to lean up against him, but she carefully moved herself a few inches away.

"Are you afraid of me?" he asked her with surprise.

"Not at all, just cautious."

"Janice, you have been telling poor Sabina terrible things about me, haven't you? I'm really quite harmless, especially when I'm injured."

Janice laughed. "Don't believe a word he says. We once saw him in a hospital with a cast up to his hip, and they still had to pry the nurses away from him."

Sabina had never been quite this close to Miguel, never so acutely aware of the dramatic impact of his features. It was a narrow face honed to a rugged texture from a lifetime of daily contact with the sun and the elements. His thick dark hair, sprinkled with silver, was at the moment unkempt, falling onto his forehead above the straight slashes of his dark eyebrows. She was surprised at his absurdly long lashes, which were tinged golden on the tips from the sun. He had a slight scar on his upper lip, which drew her attention to the sensuous way it curved, especially when he smiled.

"Tell me how you did in the race after I left you," he said.

"I finished fourth." Why were the words starting to stick in the back of her throat?

"She would have won," offered Paul, "but her horse hurdled the gate tracks at the eighth pole and lost ground."

"He's done that kind of thing before," said Miguel. "I wonder why Lathrop doesn't try him with blinkers."

Sabina was amazed that he would remember such a detail about a rather insignificant horse, but then she'd heard that he had an encyclopedic knowledge of race horses. In the jockey's room he was always coming up with obscure statistics about various thoroughbreds.

With so many jockeys around, the conversation quickly turned to the results of the day's races. It was certainly a subject to which Sabina could contribute, but Miguel had slowly managed to place himself by her again, and the warmth of his body was giving her an uncharacteristic shyness.

As soon as some other people joined the party, she started to get up from the bed, but Miguel slipped his hand up under her long hair and held her in place.

"Stay," he said in a low voice. "You cannot imagine what you're doing for the pain." It was the same tone of voice he had used to coax Composure into the starting gate, and like the recalcitrant Composure, she found it impossible to refuse him.

His strong fingers began to massage the muscles in her neck. "Tight," he commented, and kneaded harder. "That hurt?" he asked when he saw her wince. She nodded. "Then it's doing some good. Don't complain."

"Did you hear me complain?"

He grinned at her. "Not a word. You're a brave girl. Ah, there goes that knot. Do you feel it?"

She did and suddenly felt more relaxed. Even her tongue untied itself. "Miguel, you are a magician, a psychiatrist, an excellent masseur and not a bad jockey. I'd recommend you to anyone."

"Very generous of you." He kissed her on the cheek, and the touch of lips on her skin briefly brought back all the old premassage symptoms. To her horror, she even felt her face flush. She hadn't had that kind of reaction to a kiss since she was in her teens.

Reeling from the tumult inside her chest, she hardly noticed that the room had grown oddly silent. Following everyone's gaze, she realized why.

With the kind of entrance she supposed could only be orchestrated by a prima ballerina, Natasha Ivanov floated into the room.

Chapter 2

NATASHA'S LONG BLOND HAIR WAS SWEPT UP OFF her slender neck in a manner that might have been mistaken as careless, but it was done so alluringly, with slightly curled wisps framing her oval face, that she must have taken time with it. Her filmy pale-blue dress floated around her tiny dancer's body as she moved toward the bed.

Any minute now I'm going to hear Tchaikovsky violins, mused Sabina, and Natasha is going to execute a grand jeté into the center of the bed, bouncing me onto the floor.

Sabina started to rise, but Miguel's strong hand held her in place. Natasha caught the slight gesture, and for the first time took a good look at the woman sitting beside her lover on the bed.

Sabina suddenly knew how it felt to be a filly up for auction. Natasha scrutinized her so thorough-

ly that Sabina wondered momentarily if she'd
open her mouth to check her teeth. The Russian
ballerina was too regal and self-assured to appear
jealous, if indeed she was. Instead she smiled
warmly, extended a hand and said, "Hello, I'm
Natasha Ivanov. I don't believe we've met before."

"Allow me to introduce you," Miguel broke in.
"Natasha, this is my friend Sabina Martin. She
races with me at the track."

"You're a jockey?" Natasha regarded her with
surprise and a lightning reappraisal. "What an
interesting profession for a woman. Are there
many of you?"

"Nationwide, about two hundred."

"As opposed to how many men?"

"About four thousand."

"How fascinating," noted Natasha. "And it is
perhaps the only professional sport where women
compete directly against men."

"On their own turf, so to speak," added Sabina.

Miguel laughed, but Natasha, who had not
caught the pun, didn't. So Sabina explained.

She was not in a good position to judge Miguel's expression, since she was seeing him in
profile, but Natasha's feelings were obvious.
Sabina was staring at a woman who was madly,
passionately, possessively in love. How devastat-
ing it must be to see another woman beside him
on the bed where, no doubt, they had spent many
a torrid night together. She couldn't stop herself
from imagining the beauty of their two exquisitely
honed bodies entwined there, firelight reflecting
off their skin. The film reel of her thoughts made

her feel uncomfortably like a voyeur and she started once again to rise.

This time Miguel not only held her there but said, "No, stay here."

A muscle in Natasha's graceful neck tightened, but still maintaining her dignity, she sat down on the bed at Miguel's feet. "How is your ankle?" she asked.

"Much better," he said pleasantly, and continued to massage Sabina's neck, but it was the absentminded kind of stroking he might give a horse, no longer the concentrated massage of one dedicated to untying knots.

Suddenly Sabina understood the role she was being asked to play in this little bedroom farce. Miguel was either trying to make Natasha jealous or to put her off.

Still smarting from Frank's use of her that afternoon to impress Gusty's owner, Sabina was in no mood to be used again, especially to make another woman miserable. Tough years at racetracks had convinced her that women had enough trouble in life from men without tripping each other up. This time she stood up with purpose and gave Miguel a cold smile that signaled the end of the game.

"Excuse me," she said to Natasha, "I'm going to get a drink. May I bring you back something?"

"No thank you, dear, but it is very kind of you to offer." Kind to offer to leave the bed, Sabina knew she meant. The two women understood each other. The ballerina looked relieved and grateful.

After picking up a drink from the bar and taking a delicious seafood hors d'oeuvre from a tray the maid was passing around, she joined Paul, Janice and Bardy by the fireplace.

Bardy was a former jockey turned trainer, a small wiry man with a tan, weathered face. Because of a limp from an injury that had forced him into retirement, he walked with a cane.

"You got a lot out of that colt this afternoon," he said to her. "More'n anybody thought he was capable of."

She thanked him for the compliment. Coming from one of the top trainers in the country, it was a remark she wished she could record and play back to Frank Lathrop.

As they talked about the race she glanced over at the bed. She had been wrong to think the tension between Natasha and Miguel would be resolved once she removed herself. As Miguel must have predicted, the voltage only increased with the buffer gone. There were none of the nips and kicks of two horses sparring, but it looked no less dangerous. Everyone else in the room had moved politely out of earshot as the two talked animatedly. It was interesting to note that Natasha had not taken the place Sabina had vacated beside him but remained a short distance away.

Janice was checking her watch. "Honey," she said to her husband, "we'd better get home and check on Chloe."

"We've got a sick child at home," Paul told her, "but if you'd like to stay longer, I'm sure you could hitch a ride with someone. Had no idea this was going to be a party. Leave it to Carrasco."

"I'd just as soon go with you," she said. "I've got to be down at the track at five thirty in the morning to exercise horses." Since she couldn't support herself yet on the money she made as a jockey, she supplemented her income as an exercise rider.

A few years before, even that profession had been closed to women at San Felipe. But slowly women had moved in and done well at it, though the same trainers who gladly used women to exercise their horses declined to put them in a race. "Horses need a light hand in the morning, but you wouldn't have the strength when it comes to the race," was their usual excuse.

"Stop by the barn in the morning," said Bardy. "I've got some horses I'd like you to breeze for me, if you've got the time."

"Will do," she said eagerly. "Thanks." Although she had been by his barn several times, he had never asked her to work his horses before. In fact, he was one of the few trainers who still did not use exercise girls regularly. It was not like being asked to race his horses, but it was a foot in the door of a prestigious stable.

Patience, she told herself for the hundredth time. It wasn't going to come overnight. It hadn't been easy getting established in the Midwest, either, but she'd done it.

She went with Janice and Paul back over to Miguel's bed to say good night.

"Your goddaughter is sick," Janice told him, "so we've got to get home."

A worried look crossed his face. "Is it serious?"

"One of those kid things," said Paul, "but you know Janice. Chloe sneezes, and she's ready to call an ambulance."

"I'll call her tomorrow," promised Miguel.

"And I'll send her something. What would she like?"

"I don't think there's anything you haven't already given her," said Janice. "But a phone call would be terrific. You two can commiserate from your sickbeds."

Miguel turned to Sabina. "Why are you going so early? Do you also have a sneezing child at home?"

"No. But I have to be down at the track early."

He took her hand, and she felt the electricity shoot down to her toes again. "I appreciate your coming by tonight, Sabina. Do you race tomorrow?"

"Not unless I get lucky. I'm just exercising."

"Then why don't you come by here when you're through? We'll have lunch."

Natasha's French perfume seemed to increase in strength. Sabina couldn't even bear to look at her.

"Uh, I don't know. . . ."

"Call me when you're done with workouts in the morning and let me know." Did he sense the reason for her hesitation? The invitation seemed particularly callous, with Natasha sitting there. Was there a streak of ruthlessness in Miguel Carrasco that she hadn't suspected before?

However, on the drive back to her apartment, she wondered if she wasn't reading too much into his invitation. It could be that he was just being friendly to a new jockey. If she were a male jockey, she would see it that way.

And yet there had been something undefinable in the depths of his dark eyes that disturbed her. She wondered if she should accept his invitation.

It was still dark out when she arrived at the track at five thirty. She had always liked a track at that hour. The grandstands were empty, and there was a mysterious chill in the air, a quiet prelude to the excitement of the afternoons.

The thoroughbreds were hanging their heads out of their stalls, nickering, pawing the ground. They'd had their ration of grain earlier and knew the hay would not come until they'd been out for exercise.

An average racehorse was only out of his stall for around forty-five minutes a day when he was not racing: a few minutes running around the track, then cooling out at a walk. For a huge animal, primed on the best food and vitamins, conditioned as an athlete, motion was natural and eagerly anticipated.

After thinking things through Sabina decided to try to make amends with Frank. It didn't mean she had to compromise any principles, but a little humility might let her continue racing.

She noted wryly that Gusty Guy had been moved to the stall closest to the tack room. It was the stall reserved for the "star" horse, a location where the trainer could better keep an eye on him. Frank hadn't been willing to compliment her in front of Gusty's owner, but he had obviously been impressed with the horse's performance yesterday. Gusty leaned his head out of the stall and nickered at her.

"Good morning, Gusty." She patted his neck, and he nuzzled her. She genuinely liked the colt, and was sure his affectionate response had something to do with the way he ran for her. "No, we won't be going out to gallop this morning. You need to rest up from yesterday."

Hearing her voice, Frank came out of his office, a cup of coffee in hand. "Didn't your agent call you?" There was a sharp edge of sarcasm in his voice.

"Look, Frank, let's talk this out. I'll admit I lost my temper yesterday, but there was no reason to put down my riding."

"If you were a better rider, I wouldn't have to."

Was this worth it? She took a deep breath and gave one more stab. "Well, I'd like to make amends."

"Having trouble getting mounts, are you?"

The humility wasn't worth it. "Oh, ride your own damn horses, Frank," she said, and turned away, nearly bumping into Patsy Dimpton.

"Hi, guys. Which horse would you like me to work today, Frank?" Patsy Dimpton was a pert eighteen-year-old who had shown up at the track a few weeks before, looking for work as an exercise rider. Since she didn't have a license yet, some of the trainers, including Frank, had been giving her horses to "hot walk" or cool off after exercising and racing.

"Uh, start with Spare Parts," said Frank, and turned back into his office.

Sabina turned toward Patsy. "Hey, congratulations. When did you get your exercise license?"

"Just yesterday."

"That was quick."

"I got friendly with an outrider," said Patsy, "if you know what I mean."

"You don't have to get *that* friendly with them," said Sabina with concern. "As long as you can ride, they'll okay you for a license."

Outriders were the patrolmen of the track. When a rider was on a runaway horse, or in some kind of trouble, it was the outrider who rushed in to help. When someone wanted to get an exercise license, an outrider checked out their riding ability and reported back to the stewards.

Patsy shrugged philosophically.

"I talked to some of the girls, and they said dating an outrider was the quickest way to a license. Otherwise, you can hang around here as a hot walker for months, maybe years, before you even get promoted to groom, which is even worse. Who wants to muck out stalls and clean tack? I want to be a jockey. I can't afford to waste that much time."

Sabina was all for increasing the number of women jockeys, but she frowned on the easy shortcuts. She herself had worked her way up slowly as hot walker, groom, then exercise girl. Most jockeys, men and women, paid their dues this way, and the system gave them invaluable knowledge of every aspect of thoroughbred care.

But she was not about to waste her breath lecturing Patsy. It was her experience that when kids were that anxious to ride, they rarely listened to advice. For women it was much tougher to get started than for men. She had never done it, but she couldn't condemn a girl for being desperate enough to use her body now and then to get a leg up. It was really the men who were to blame for holding sex over these girls.

No matter what else she thought of Frank, although he had dropped some annoying innuendos into conversation, he had never made sex a condition for riding his horses. He had a number of women working for him as grooms and exercise girls.

"I'm glad Frank is giving you a chance to ride," said Sabina, knowing how difficult it was even to get exercise mounts at San Felipe.

"He was easier than the outrider," she said with a sigh. "Only one night."

Sabina felt the glow of anger on her cheeks. "That bastard," she murmured.

"Oh, no," said Patsy nervously. "You weren't serious about Frank or anything, were you? I mean, I just figured it was business for you, too. I wouldn't want to . . ."

"Frank doesn't mean anything to me, and I've never done anything for him but ride his horses. I just think he was a bastard, like the outrider, for using sex as leverage over you."

She walked back into Frank's office and slammed the door behind her. "Frank, Patsy's only eighteen years old! Just out of high school. You're a good-looking man. You don't need to get it like that."

He chewed on the end of a pencil, then flung it across the desk. "Patsy Dimpton's eighteen going on fifty. She knew what she was getting into."

"Damn it, think about what you just said. You've got a daughter that age!" She tapped the framed photograph on his desk.

He glared at her belligerently. "That halo

pinching your brain and making your vision a little hazy, Sabina? You've been around tracks a few years. Just who uses whom? I used to work the fair ground circuit and went out with a lot of you girl jockeys. Just as soon as another trainer comes along with a better horse, you're off like a flash."

"I've ridden for a lot of trainers," she said with disgust. "And, thank God, most of them care more about how you perform on a horse than on how you perform in the sack. In spite of all your yelling, Frank, I really thought you were a pretty good guy. I would have expected it of a lot of trainers, but not you."

She stormed out the door and down the steps, still seething with rage, but trying to pull herself together.

Gusty nickered at her again. She walked over and leaned her head against his and scratched his shoulders. Ever since she was a child, horses had provided a tranquil refuge. It never failed that after a few minutes with a friendly horse, she calmed down. "I'll miss you, Gusty Guy. Maybe that idiot will put blinkers on you next time so you won't leap over the gate tracks."

She gave Gusty a final pat and walked to the end of the barn, where the groom was giving Patsy a leg up. Patsy landed like a sack of potatoes on the horse's back. Startled by the sudden weight, Spare Parts danced to the side before Patsy could get settled, and she fell off.

"Patsy, let me show you the correct way to do that," said Sabina. "Put your weight on your hands as you go down, and lower yourself lightly so you don't startle him."

Patsy tried it a few more times and finally got it right. "Hey, thanks, Sabina. I've mounted a lot of horses. It didn't occur to me this was any different."

Sabina didn't even want to think about what else Patsy didn't know. If she was smart, she'd pick it up. If not, she'd end up flat on her back again, but this time it wouldn't be in a trainer or outrider's bed.

People were always drawing parallels to the casting couch, but if an actress couldn't act, she only made a fool of herself in front of a camera. On the track, if a woman couldn't ride, she risked nothing less than her life.

Sabina was upset, but she refused to let it get her down. There had been times she'd fallen off in the middle of a race and been trampled under by five horses. And there was that time in Colorado with Al. Nothing had been worse than that. Frank Lathrop was just another setback. It wasn't the end of the world. If she'd learned anything, it was to keep her head, and keep going.

One could tell the kind of trainer Bardy was by the way his barns were kept. Lush green lawns were planted in front of his lengthy shed row, which housed close to forty horses. On the lawn were white wrought-iron chairs and jockey statues. Boxes of small trees, bushes and flowers lined the walkways.

"All those pink petunias don't make the horses run any better," Frank had observed when Sabina had suggested he might do something similar to spruce up his own barn.

"Maybe not, but potential owners are going to figure that if you take care of your barn that well, you're going to do the same with their horses. Besides, you spend fourteen, fifteen hours a day here, you might as well make it pleasant."

Bardy Mulligan even had a sun pen outside his stable, which Sabina thought was particularly innovative. She'd always felt a little sorry for race horses, who spent so much time cooped up in a stall. The pen gave them an opportunity, for at least a half hour a day, to stand in the sun and roll around in the sand if they liked. The petunias might not help, but horses that were happier were bound to run better.

Bardy was watching a groom wrap a horse's leg when she found him. "I'd like to put you on Xenophon today," he told her. "He likes a light hand. Nobody's been on him since he won his race last week with Carrasco. He was a little sore after the race, but seems to be over it now. Just keep him at an easy hobbyhorse once around the track, and let me know what you think."

Sabina found it hard to mask her excitement. In all her years of riding, she had never been on a horse as good as Xenophon. A big, rangy three-year-old, who had won or placed in the last five races, he was a leading candidate, along with Composure, for the $500,000 San Felipe Derby.

Anxious to get out on the track and run, Xenophon barely stood still while the groom gave her a leg up. He tossed his head, kicked his legs out behind him, and even gave her a friendly little buck for good measure.

The pony rider, a heavy-set girl named Bonnie,

came up to her on her horse and grabbed Xenophon's rein to lead her onto the track. "He's in good spirits, today."

"Sure is," Sabina agreed enthusiastically. "A lot of horse, this one."

"Hey, would you take a look at who's exercising," said Bonnie with a raucous laugh. "Little Patsy's finally got herself a license. Look at the way she's flopping around in the saddle, her legs swingin' back and forth like pendulums. God knows how many outriders she had to sleep with to get that license. One of those creeps is going to feel pretty silly in a minute when he has to go over and pick her up out of the dirt. I wonder which trainer had an itch that needed scratching last night."

"Frank Lathrop," supplied one of the exercise boys, who was on a horse beside them. It didn't take long for word to travel down the shed-row telegraph.

Bonnie was looking at her, gauging her response. Sabina knew that everyone probably assumed she had been sleeping with Frank, too.

Her attention was suddenly riveted to the track. "Oh, no!" Sabina gasped. "What's Patsy doing riding up on the rail like that when somebody's working a horse?"

Bonnie groaned. "The stupid fool!"

The two women watched in horror as the jockey came up behind Patsy and shouted "Inside!" meaning that she should move out of the way.

"Patsy didn't even turn around to look!" Bonnie cried. The rider was forced to make a dangerous swerve, losing precious time and nearly bumping another horse.

"Tell me that's not going to set women here at the track back about ten years," Bonnie grumbled. "Most of us work damn hard to establish some kind of credibility here, and then some little doe-eyed idiot goes out and messes it up for all of us."

"Maybe she just didn't know what you're supposed to do when somebody yells 'Inside' or 'Outside.' I didn't when I got started," said Sabina. "I'll talk to her about it. She's still got a lot to learn."

"And while she's learning, she could be killing people and horses. I saw that happen a couple of years ago. Four horses went down, broke their legs and had to be put down. One rider was in the hospital for six months. We ought to bring that kind of stuff up at the women's meeting tonight. You're going, aren't you?"

"I'll be there," said Sabina. "I've never been much of an organization person, but I think maybe at San Felipe, it's time the women got organized."

"Good, 'cause you're the only jockey we got. And if the guys see many more gals like Patsy out there, they're gonna kick us all out of here on our pretty little faces."

"Don't knock pretty little faces," said Sabina. "They seem to be the unit of exchange out here."

Bardy was not given to wordy compliments, but he was evidently pleased enough with the way she handled Xenophon to give her five more horses that morning and ask her to come back the next day.

"I'd really like to race them for you," she said.

"We'll see."

At least it wasn't a flat no. She'd exercise his horses a few more days, then have her agent call him. It was worth a try, even though realistically, she would probably have an easier time getting a mount with a trainer of Frank's caliber.

There was still something inside that made her want to tell Miguel she couldn't make it for lunch, but as soon as she heard his voice on the phone, she lost the will to refuse.

"Is there anything special you would like to have for lunch?" he asked her on the phone.

"I'll eat anything as long as it doesn't have calories."

Miguel laughed. "I know what you mean. It is a continual fight. Bring a bathing suit, if you'd like. The pool is heated, and it's like summer today."

She fished around in the back of her dresser for her bathing suit, a hot-pink bikini Al had once picked out for her. She wondered if it was wise to look so provocative when she had no desire to provoke.

But Miguel, if a bit of a rogue, was a gentleman and not likely to turn into a belligerent animal if she turned him down.

Chapter 3

THERE WAS A SLEEK CADILLAC PARKED IN THE circular driveway when she arrived. She had seen Miguel's silver gull-wing Mercedes in the parking lot at San Felipe, so she knew it wasn't his. Perhaps he had invited others for lunch. It made her feel even easier about the afternoon.

The butler, who had been serving drinks in Miguel's bedroom the night before, answered the door and said, "Mr. Carrasco is with his doctor right now. He asked me to show you in and . . ."

The voices from the living room had become too loud to ignore, and suddenly she and the butler found themselves inadvertently eavesdropping.

"You're a blithering idiot," came a booming man's voice. "You had no business checking yourself out of the hospital last night, and you have no business getting back on another one of those loony bone-busting hay burners. Enough! You've had one hell of a career. It's time to call it quits. Next accident, you might not be so lucky."

"I feel fine, Max." Miguel did not sound the least bit worried about Max's dire predictions.

"A lot you know."

"Max, what do you know? You only look at X-rays. You're a good doctor, but you have no idea what's going on inside."

"Idiocy. That's what's inside."

The two men suddenly appeared in the entry hall. The servant looked ill at ease. "Miss Martin just arrived," he said apologetically.

"And none too soon," said Miguel with a broad smile. "Let me introduce you to the eminent Dr. Backer, top orthopedic surgeon in Los Angeles, who thinks I am a blithering idiot."

"Blithering," agreed Dr. Backer. He was a muscular bear of a man with a generous smile and a cap of silver hair.

"Miss Martin hardly knows me," said Miguel, "so she hasn't had much chance to form an opinion on the matter of my idiocy."

"Take my word for it," grumbled Max. "If you were my daughter, I'd warn you to stay away from any man who rides thoroughbred race horses for a living."

"That would be difficult for Sabina," said Miguel. "She's also a jockey."

"Then you're probably as wacko as he is."

"It's a prerequisite for entering the profession," she said.

Dr. Backer shook his head. "Well, young lady, I hope I don't see you as often as I see the rest of those San Felipe daredevils. My advice would be to stay away from the horses, unless you're betting on them, and get married to some nice guy. Definitely not this one. Miguel, would you at least come by the hospital tomorrow so we can complete the X-rays?"

"I'll think about it," promised Miguel. "Are you sure you can't stay for lunch, Max?"

"No, I've got an appointment with a crazy linebacker this afternoon. Athletes," he grumbled. "A bunch of self-destructive blithering idiots. I could be talking to myself. You never listen to me."

"We keep you in business, Max."

"Better I should have been a dermatologist, like my mother wanted. None of these frustrations. People with skin problems don't have delusions of immortality to contend with."

Smiling at Sabina, Miguel led her through an elaborate game room, complete with pool table, poker table and bar, and out through tall French doors, across a long expanse of sloping lawn and gardens to an Olympic-size swimming pool. At the far end of the pool was a large bathhouse with a tropical lanai large enough to hold a few hundred people for a party.

"You can change in here." He pointed the way toward a bedroom. "Meet you outside in a minute. What are you drinking?"

"Just ice water."

He raised his eyebrows. "Are you sure you can afford the calories?"

When she emerged from the bathhouse, she saw that Miguel had ignored the chaise longues and was stretched out on a towel on the grass. He was wearing blue swim trunks, and just as it had last night, her pulse raced at seeing his tan, muscled body. Today, caressed by the winter sun's slanting golden rays, she felt breathless with desire.

When he saw her, he started to get up. A slight creasing at the corners of his eyes told her the effort caused him pain. There was a bandage wrapped around his ankle. He had been limping badly as he led her down to the pool. She thought about what Dr. Backer had said.

The look of pain left his dark eyes as his irreverent gaze swept over her, taking in the hot-pink bikini and what it barely covered.

Aside from extremely well-developed pectoral muscles and shoulders, Sabina considered herself to be in possession of a rather unremarkable body. Barely five feet, she had small breasts, narrow hips and the leg muscles of a dancer. It was a rather boyish figure, she thought, lacking in the soft, undulant curves a poet would compose odes to, but a body perfectly suited to her line of work.

Miguel had an expressive face. It was obvious he approved of what he saw. Of course, he had been enthralled with a ballerina's body, too. Probably some quirk had given him a taste for women with muscles, she surmised.

"Take one of the lounges if you like, or bring a towel over here. I always prefer the grass to the plastic foam of those things."

The grass did sound more inviting, though she wasn't sure what would happen if she lay there beside Miguel.

"Would you like to take a swim before lunch?"

"You'll join me in the pool?"

"Max would not approve." He looked down at the bandages around his ankle and frowned. "But to hell with Max."

He pulled himself up and hobbled toward the edge of the pool.

"Do you really think you should?" she asked with alarm.

"Max is right. I never listen to him. A few years ago he had me encased in a cast that prevented my doing much of anything I liked. So I cut it off."

"Why do you bother to consult him if you persist in ignoring him?"

"I like him. He's one of the few authentic curmudgeons left in a world overburdened with Pollyannas."

"He thinks you should quit riding?"

"Max thinks *you* should quit riding," said Miguel lightly. "And you didn't even have an accident. He thinks anything more dangerous than walking from a car to a restaurant is blithering idiocy." He took her hand and led her to the end of the pool. "Come on, I'll race you the length."

"Race? Miguel, your ankle!"

He looked down at it as though it were an extra piece of weight attached to his saddle. "You're right," he said after a moment. "You'd better give me a head start to even up the odds."

Before she could protest, he made a dive into the pool, slicing the water with barely a splash. She was in the water seconds after him, the racing instinct in her as strong as any thoroughbred's.

She didn't have a chance against him, even with his bad ankle.

"That wasn't fair," she complained when they reached the end. "I can see you're definitely not to be trusted." She floated on her back and gazed up at the cloudless blue sky.

"All right," he said reasonably. "It won't do for you not to trust me so early in our relationship. I'll race you back. This time fairly."

She gazed at him askance.

"I promise," he said.

She had been on the swim team in high school, and had even considered training seriously for competition. This time she gave him a run for his money.

When he reached the end of the pool, he pulled himself out, sat on the edge and shook his head free of water. "You are good! You swim as well as you ride."

"There was a time I took swimming as seriously as I do horse racing. Did you ever go out for other sports?"

"I play a little golf now, but when I was young, it was always the horses."

"You're such a superb athlete, though. You didn't go out for track or anything in high school?"

He threw his head back and turned his face to the sun. "I never went to high school."

"Oh, I'd forgotten. You're from South America. The educational system must be different."

"At thirteen my schooling was interrupted. And I went straight to the track."

He stood up and started back to the grass. His

limp was worse now. It had been crazy of him to push himself. He was like a thoroughbred that continued to run a race on a broken leg.

Once again she was acutely aware of the beauty of his athlete's body: the powerful shoulders, the back muscles tapering to his waist, the strong legs. She found it impossible not to appreciate a man's well-formed body—or that of any animal that was at its peak. She thought of the racehorses that morning, the rippling taut muscles as they ran, the silky manes and tails flowing in the wind created from their own speed.

Not ready yet to relinquish the satiny feel of the water against her skin, she swam a few more laps before joining him on the grass.

Her ice water, in a tall glass with a twist of lemon on the rim, was soon beside her. She took a sip, then settled back on the towel—aware that he was watching her every move, and enjoying it.

Although he had done nothing overt, his sultry gaze made her uneasy.

"Didn't your parents object to your dropping out of school?" she asked to divert his attention. It did seem unlikely that aristocratic parents would have allowed a son to drop out of school to pursue a career as a jockey.

He paused a moment before answering. "They didn't have much choice in the matter."

"I could see from the way you enjoyed flaunting Dr. Backer's authority that you must have been a model child."

He smiled, but there was a dark flickering in his eyes that warned her she had inadvertently touched on a painful subject. "Did your parents mind that you became a jockey?" she asked cautiously.

"My father," he began slowly, "made the unfortunate choice of supporting the losing side of a nasty little revolution. I was the youngest of four brothers, spared because I was too young to fight. The only one of my family. Everyone else, including my mother, was killed."

Sabina was temporarily without words. The Miguel Carrasco she knew from the track had such an easy smile and joking manner. She would never have guessed there'd been a tragedy in his past.

"How did you become a jockey, then?"

"We had a ranch. At that age I knew nothing but horses. My brothers and I used to race across the meadows. Since there was no horse racing in my country, I went to Panama, where I started as a stable boy. The year I was the top jockey in Panama, an American trainer brought me to this country."

"I'm sorry about your family," she said, regretting she had been so flip about them earlier.

"Don't be, Sabina." He touched her cheek. "It would be dangerous for a woman like you."

She gave him a confused look. "I don't understand what is so dangerous about a little sympathy."

"You could confuse your emotions. You are very sensitive, Sabina. That almost psychic ability to communicate on an emotional level with a horse makes you a superb jockey. Sympathy is a dangerously seductive emotion. I won't seduce you that way."

"You want to seduce me?" she blurted out clumsily. The turn of conversation had taken her by surprise.

The heavy eyelids lowered as his gaze dropped to her lips. "Very much. If we make love, it must be because you are burning with the need, not because you want to cure the pain of my loss."

This was obviously something he had encountered before. With Natasha?

"Miguel, I appreciate all the warning signals, but they're really not necessary. I have no desire at the moment to get involved in a love affair. I think the best solution is for us just to be friends. Then I can feel all the sympathy I want and you don't have to worry about my being seduced for all the wrong reasons."

"That sounds to me like an excellent suggestion," he said, leaning back on the grass to rest on his elbows. "I would very much like you as a friend."

She was slightly disappointed at his easy capitulation, but relieved.

"You have beautiful skin, *mi bonita*," he ran a hand down her arm. "But I am afraid you are going to get sunburned out here. Let me get you some lotion."

"No, you stay off that ankle," she said. "Just tell me where it is, and I'll bring it out here."

"In the medicine cabinet in the bathhouse," he told her.

She was aware of his gaze on her as she walked along the side of the pool, and once again, it made her self-conscious. Was there any part of his magnificent body he didn't use to some effect? On the horses it was his hands and his voice; on her, those fathomless dark eyes that turned her insides to jelly.

She returned with the lotion and sank back down next to him on the grass.

"You have to be careful here in the winter," he said as he watched her apply the lotion to her legs. "There is no smog cover to keep out the ultraviolet rays. On a day like this, you could sunburn."

"I don't usually burn too badly," she said. "One of the joys of olive skin."

"Yes, we both have that. It is a blessing if you like the sun." He took the bottle from her. "Here, turn over, I'll get your back."

She rolled onto her stomach and felt the cool squirt of liquid between her shoulder blades, then the warm hand, callused from a lifetime of gripping leather reins. He rubbed slowly, in no hurry to spread the lotion.

Sabina pulled her long, damp hair up and out of the way, and he unhooked her bikini top. She started to protest, then decided he was just being thoughtful about not getting the oil on her suit. After all, the decision had been reached to be friends.

"Those muscles are still very tight," he observed as his fingers pressed into her neck.

"Occupational hazard," she murmured. She had once heard a trainer say, "Miguel Carrasco has fingers like diamonds." She was beginning to see why. They seemed to know just the right way to coax the knots loose and spread a sense of well-being through her.

"You told me you rode Bardy Mulligan's horses today," he said. "Which ones?"

"Xenophon."

"Ah! Wonderful horse, extraordinary horse."

"I kept him at an easy pace, but you could just tell from the feel of him what he was capable of. I'd love to race a horse like that one day."

"You will."

Both his hands were working on her back, circling and rubbing like those of a professional masseur. She was drifting off into a lovely euphoria as his fingers pulled, pushed and caressed. As his hands on her rib cage came close to her breasts, brushing the edges of them, it was impossible not to think about the kind of lover he would be. No wonder Natasha was loathe to lose him.

"Xenophon still sore?" If moving his hands all over her responsive body was having any effect on him, his voice didn't betray it.

"There was a little heat in his right leg when I brought him in, but it wasn't anything to worry about." Her own voice, she thought, sounded a little breathless.

His hands moved down her legs with large sweeping motions, to her toes, taking each one separately, then pressed the balls of her feet and her heels. It had never before occurred to her that the feet could be an erogenous zone, but Miguel was proving her wrong.

Everywhere he touched now his hands sent sparks back to the shimmering central core of her sexuality. His hands stroked her legs, kneading and pulling at the long muscles, moving slowly up to her thighs. She could scarcely control her breathing, afraid he would notice.

"How does that feel?" he asked.

She gulped. "Terrific."

"Good." His fingers circled the sensitive insides of her thighs, thumbs pressing dangerously close to the elastic leg bands of her bikini.

She shut her eyes, hoping she wouldn't be forced to make a conscious decision to tell him to stop.

"You're tensing up, Sabina. Relax." He shook her leg gently.

It was what you would tell a horse at the beginning of a race. Would there be a race?

"Relax, Sabina," he repeated.

Like Composure, she could only obey. "That's better." He started on her other leg.

Was he playing with her? He had to know that she was being driven slowly mad by what he was doing. And yet he wasn't using it to any advantage. At least not yet. Maybe he did really want her to relax the hard, overworked muscles.

When he finished her right leg, he gave her thigh a playful slap. "There you are, *mi bonita*. Would you like me to do the front half of you now?"

"No, that was really more than I'd bargained for," she said with difficulty.

"There were moments I thought you would tell me to stop, but it was a wise decision to let me continue," he said. "When we do make love, I shall already know a great deal about your body and what gives it pleasure."

"Miguel, I thought we decided . . ."

"Of course. Not this afternoon. I invited you to lunch, and here it is."

The maid and butler were descending the path from the house, bearing lunch on silver trays.

"Would you like to eat at the table," he asked, "or picnic style on the grass?"

"I don't think I could move after that massage," she said with a sly grin. "Let's stay here. I love picnics."

Sabina had been to a fair number of picnics in her time, but none quite like the one that was spread out before them on a white lace Belgian linen tablecloth with matching napkins in monogrammed silver napkin rings.

There was a fresh seafood salad served in a cut-glass and silver salad bowl. The imported French wine, kept chilled in a silver cooler, was poured into delicate crystal goblets. It occurred to her that there was not a thing in front of her, including the silverware, that could be tossed with reckless abandon into a dishwasher. If this was the picnic-wear, what did he use at dinner parties?

It wasn't the first time she had considered the potential financial rewards of her profession. There were, of course, only a handful of jockeys in the world who lived like this—or who even knew how—but it was possible.

She was closer to this kind of life-style at San Felipe than she'd ever been in her life. One day she too might be sitting by her own Olympic-size pool, having a picnic on bone china. No. The pool perhaps, and a picnic, but she couldn't ever see herself risking anything but unbreakable plastic by a pool. It went against her practical middle-class upbringing.

"Are you racing tomorrow?" he asked.

"Just exercising."

"Who else do you ride for at San Felipe beside Frank Lathrop?"

"So far, just Lathrop," she said. "It's a rough track to get going on. I was pretty well established in the Midwest, but out here that doesn't count for much."

"When do you ride for Frank next?"

"I'm . . . uh, well, it's possible I won't be riding for him again."

Miguel studied her closely. "You had a disagreement?"

She stabbed a crab leg with her fork. "You could call it that."

"I don't mean to be prying into your personal life."

"I didn't think anybody at a racetrack had a personal life. Everything is public domain. Anyway, there's nothing personal or mysterious about it. Frank didn't like the way I handled Gusty Guy yesterday, and he no longer wants me on his horses."

Miguel looked incredulous. "You've taken horses that should never have been entered in some races and brought them in to place. He'd be a fool to take you off them." Miguel pinned her with his dark eyes. "Frank Lathrop isn't the best trainer in the world, but he's no fool. What really happened?"

"Well, we had a disagreement," she admitted.

He studied her for a moment, the way he might study a horse he suspected of lameness, then asked, "Are you in love with him?"

"For someone who doesn't want to pry," she said acidly, "that's a pretty direct question."

"You don't have to answer it."

"This may shock you, but Frank and I aren't even dating."

Miguel's dark eyebrows raised. "Why should it shock me?"

"Because of the way everyone thinks," she said with a sigh. "Don't deny it. Why else would you ask if I was in love with him?"

"For two reasons. First of all, Lathrop let it be known around the track that you were more than his jockey."

Just when she thought she'd heard the worst about Frank, something else surfaced. All the anger she had managed to suppress earlier now came out. "Go on; what's the second reason? I can't wait to hear it."

"Several jockeys have asked you out, and you turned them all down. They all assumed the reason was that you were going with Frank."

"What egos! I don't suppose it would enter their minds, hounded as they are by fawning jockey chasers, that I just wasn't interested."

"Has your agent gotten you any new mounts?" he asked, getting back to business.

"Oh, he's been wonderfully helpful," she said bitterly. "He suggested I try seducing some trainers."

Miguel filled her crystal goblet with wine. "Don't worry. You're a good rider. Things will open up for you."

"I wish I were as certain. I'd like to stay out here in California, but I want to ride, not sit in the grandstands watching. You must know how that feels, being laid up and all."

He nodded and looked absently at the trees across the pool. She sensed what he was thinking.

"Miguel, about what Dr. Backer said. . . ."

A defiant muscle in his jaw tightened at the mention of it.

"What will you do when you quit racing?" she asked him.

"*If* I quit," he corrected her.

"If Dr. Backer is really that adamant, maybe you ought to consider it. Nothing is so important that you should risk your life."

He took her hand and raised it to his lips. "If you truly believed that, Sabina, you yourself would never take a horse into the starting gate."

"But the fact is, we can't do this forever," she argued. "Retirement is something that just has to be faced."

"Like death?"

"Don't be so morbid, Miguel! You've had a career like few jockeys in the world. You would be quitting at the top of your profession. There are a lot of things you could do to be around racing. Breed horses or train them. With your skill, you'd make a magnificent trainer."

He ran a hand across her cheek and into her hair. "You're right. I am being too morbid. And at this moment, lying here beside you, I feel very much alive."

He traced a fingertip across her eyebrows, down her cheek and over her lips. "We will be very good together."

Her throat was too dry to utter a word. She was

mesmerized by his midnight dark eyes. His gaze dropped to her breasts then went back to her lips.

The alarms were going off. She wanted to jump up and dive back into the pool. Instead, her lips parted slightly in anticipation of his kiss.

He was not going to rush it. Her anticipation swelled as he moved slowly toward her, gazing into her eyes. When their lips did touch, it was electric. She felt the meltdown in her depths.

Sun-warmed skin touched sun-warmed skin, sending waves of heat up her legs and through her body. It had been so long since Al. And even at its best, their lovemaking had never been like this.

That stark admission made her feel so guilty, she broke away.

Unwilling to end the embrace abruptly, he trailed feathery kisses down her slender neck to her shoulder. She trembled.

"Were you lying to me about Frank?" he asked softly.

It made her angry that he would question her integrity. "What makes you think I was lying?"

"The way you just pulled away from me. You act like a woman terrified to commit an act of betrayal."

The sensitivity he had attributed to her was also part of his makeup. He had correctly read her motivation, but had pinned it on the wrong source.

"Did it occur to you that perhaps I just don't want to make love to you?"

He ran a hand down her neck, stopping on her breast. Over the material of her bikini, his fingers rubbed very slightly, just enough to make her arch to him and catch her breath.

"Not once this afternoon has that occurred to me," he said and, having made his point, removed his hand. "But I am thinking that your earlier suggestion was very wise. I would like to have you as a friend. I leave the choice to you. What do you think, Sabina? Do you want to be my friend or my lover?"

Once again she was taken aback that he was willing to concede the battle so easily. Perhaps that kiss had not had the same effect on him. She had been a long time out of practice with such things.

Curious at his response, she slid the palm of her hand down his hard, muscled chest, her fingers fanning out delicately through the course black chest hair and stopping provocatively at the waistband of his swim trunks.

"What are you and Natasha," she asked, "friends or lovers?"

He looked at the spot where her hand rested, then back into her eyes, still without touching her. "Natasha is no longer a friend."

"But still a lover?"

"Is that what is bothering you?"

She toyed with the waistband. "I was an only child, Miguel, I never learned to share."

He smiled, but still did not touch her. "So you would not want to make love to me unless I could assure you there was no other woman in my life?"

"Is that what Natasha wants from you?"

"No." He brushed her smooth cheek with the

backs of his fingers. "Natasha wants more. I am asking what you want."

She drew in her breath. "I think it's best we stay friends."

"All right, *querida*," he said. "We will be friends, very good friends, I think."

An afternoon breeze came up and reminded her that it was getting late. "I'd better be going."

"What are you doing tonight?"

"There's a meeting of all the women who work at San Felipe."

"Planning an armed takeover?" he asked with amusement.

"It's not a bad idea. I'll bring it up. We were just going to do sweet little feminine things like sip alfalfa tea and embroider our horse blankets."

He was walking with more difficulty as he showed her to the front door.

"I'm glad you came this afternoon, Sabina."

"Me too," she said sincerely. "I'm glad we're friends."

He encircled her small waist and gazed into her eyes. "We will be more," he said, and kissed her lightly on the lips. "Much more in time."

The touch of his lips kindled the fire within her again, but she was determined to resist. Her physical needs were one thing, but his friendship was really all she could handle right now. It was a relief that the afternoon had turned out the way it had.

It would be a long time before she was able to commit herself again. And she was determined it would not be to another jockey. As attractive and appealing as they were, there was always that lurking potential for heartbreak and tragedy.

Besides, there were too many things to concentrate on at the moment without the diversion of a love affair. And a woman who loved Miguel Carrasco was bound to become, like Natasha, consumed by it.

Chapter 4

THE WOMEN WERE MEETING IN THE NEARBY HOME OF Charlotte Ficus, an assistant trainer who had organized the meeting and tacked the notices on bulletin boards. She was a tall, energetic woman who aspired to being a full trainer.

Although almost every woman who worked at the track was there, down to the clerks who sold pari-mutuel tickets, not all were in favor of forming even a loose women's organization.

"We get down there and start waving banners," said a vet assistant, who echoed the sentiments of many of the women, "and the men are going to feel intimidated and resentful."

"We're making progress here slowly," said an exercise girl, "and that's the way it should be. Five years ago you didn't see a single exercise girl. Now we've even got a jockey."

"Let's ask the jockey what she thinks," suggested Charlotte. "Do you think we need an organization, Sabina?"

Sabina shifted uncomfortably in her chair. Racing a thousand-pound horse down a muddy track in the pouring rain didn't make her as nervous as speaking in front of a group of people.

She cleared her throat. "Well, we've got to figure that the reason we're at any track is not because trainers are getting more liberated, but because they've discovered that we do a lot of jobs better and work harder than the men."

There was scattered applause, which gave her some confidence to continue. "When I was a groom, I used to have trainers tell me that some of the guys they hired would turn up drunk in a stall with a bottle in their hand. We're willing to put up with the lousy pay and poor conditions not because we can't get any other kind of a job, but because we love the horses. And I think that's what we have to impress on them."

"But what about a woman's organization?" prodded Charlotte. "How do you feel about that?"

"It depends on the organization, I guess. I tend to agree with JoAnne. Running around with picket signs isn't going to get us anywhere, but since I've been at San Felipe, I've seen a lot of the problems women are having. Maybe getting together to talk about some of them, and looking for alternative solutions, would help."

Patsy Dimpton raised her hand. "This morning I was riding my first exercise mount and I didn't know what in the world I was doing."

"You can say that again," mumbled Bonnie from the back row, sitting next to Sabina.

"Well, I'll admit it," Patsy snapped back. "But later Sabina` helped me out, showed me how to mount and told me about track courtesy. I really appreciated it. I was thinking that maybe Sabina, since she's the best rider here, could work with some of us, hold kind of a class for those of us who want to become jockeys."

Sabina scrunched down in her chair. She was all for a little coaching now and then, but teaching a full-time class was the last thing she needed to fill what little free time remained to her.

"That's a wonderful idea," said Charlotte. "What do you say, Sabina?"

"I wouldn't mind," she hedged, "but there are some excellent jockey schools around that could do a much better job."

"Do you have any idea what they cost?" said Charlotte. "Most of the women here are just barely staying alive as it is."

Sabina felt cornered. "I'd be happy to take some girls out to Griffith Park one afternoon I'm not racing and work with them, but I think this is an effort we could all contribute to. Charlotte, maybe there are some girls who'd like to learn how to be trainers, and you could hold classes for them. And Bonnie, maybe some would like to be pony riders."

With the organizational skill that served her so well as an assistant trainer, Charlotte immediately produced sign-up sheets and figured out time schedules. Sabina suddenly found herself the teacher of a class of ten hopeful Patsy Dimptons.

"This is all fine and good and damn helpful," Charlotte concluded. "But I'd still like to do something that would make those guys stand up

and take notice. Maybe get some media coverage
for us. After all, it's ridiculous that a track the size
of San Felipe has only one woman jockey riding
here, and even she has a hard time getting good
horses to ride."

Sabina wasn't going to say anything to risk
alienating Charlotte, but she couldn't help thinking that the woman was a hypocrite. As an
assistant trainer, she certainly had the power to
put a woman jockey on some horses. But as many
times as Sabina had been by her barn, Charlotte
and the trainer she worked with had always been
ready with one excuse or another.

Patsy raised her hand. "I've got an idea."

Sabina shuddered to think what new gem Patsy
would come up with next.

"How about our organizing an all-women race,
flying the best gals in here from all over the
country. I bet San Felipe would love to sponsor it.
Just think of all the publicity they'd get!"

There were rumbles of excitement about the
plan.

"Wait a minute," said Sabina. "San Felipe runs
the best horses in the world for the highest stakes.
Last Sunday they had sixty-two thousand people
packing the stands. It's not as though they're hard
up for gimmicks to get people out to the track."

"But there are a lot of other days they don't
have that many people," argued Charlotte. "The
press department might be crazy about this. I
think we ought to make an appointment with Bob
Perile and discuss it with him," she went on,
mentioning San Felipe's general manager. "It's a
hell of an idea and well worth a try."

Sabina shrugged. "If there's a chance, I'm all for it. I've got a lot of friends who'd love to come out here to race at San Felipe."

"Good, then we'll put you on the committee to see Bob Perile. How about you, too, Patsy, since it was your idea?"

Patsy was anxious to join in, thrilled to be included.

There was more discussion, including mention of the annoying demands for sexual favors in exchange for horses. Some of the women had found innovative ways to deal with the problem and were ready to share them with the others.

Sabina felt good about the meeting. The archaic attitudes about women were not going to change overnight simply because the women had formed an organization, but this was a step in the right direction. At least the women were talking and sharing ideas.

She was exhausted when she got back to her apartment that night. A day of galloping horses, baking in the sun, unburdening herself to Miguel, and now the women's meeting, left her feeling depleted.

She barely had enough time to slip out of her clothes, climb into bed and set the alarm before she began drifting off to sleep.

But lying there in bed, she began wondering what would have happened if things had taken a different turn with Miguel that afternoon. Never had she been so wildly, physically attracted to a man in her life. With Al, things had blossomed gradually.

Well, she was glad she and Miguel were going

to be friends. There was a lot she liked about him, but she remembered the way he had treated Natasha the night before. One did not discard friends as carelessly as one did lovers.

She arrived at Bardy Mulligan's barn twenty minutes early the next morning. In her experience, nothing impressed a trainer like being early. She was checking for tears on the saddle and bridle of her first mount when Bardy approached her, that afternoon's racing schedule in his hand.

"You said you wanted to ride for me?"

Her heart stopped. "I sure would."

"Well, I got a mare in the fourth race this afternoon. It's a one-mile allowance race for fillies and mares four-years-old and up. The horse is no Landaluce. But she's won some. Name's Heidi Sioux. You interested?"

Interested? She'd have ridden a tricycle if Bardy Mulligan had offered it to her. "Sure," she said calmly.

They walked down to the stall to look at the horse. "She likes to get clear out in front at the start. If you can get into a good position out of the gate, she'll run for you fine." Then he told her which horses and jockeys she'd be up against, and what kind of strategy to use if they got her hemmed in.

As soon as she finished workouts that morning, she called Miguel to tell him the good news. "You don't sound very surprised," she told him.

"I am very pleased for you," he said warmly. "I wish I could be out at the track today to see you, but I've got to be at the hospital for X-rays. Why don't you get a tape of the race, and we'll watch it together tonight. Get her out front early if you can, and keep her there."

"Thanks, Bardy told me about that."

"And another thing with that horse: She doesn't change leads very well. Last time I was on her, she almost hit the fence in the stretch."

"I'll watch out for it. What time would you like me to come over tonight?"

"Come for dinner, whenever you're through at the track. And good luck this afternoon. I know you're going to do well."

Winter weather in Southern California could be capricious when the cool, moist winds off the north Pacific swept down and drove the desert heat inland. That afternoon dark clouds were gathering at the peaks of the Santa Monica Mountains casting blue shadows onto the track. In the walking ring where the jockeys were mounting up, the horses, sensitive to the climate changes, lifted their long necks and widened their nostrils.

Sabina had an hour before she had to be in the jockey's room, so she decided to go backside to chat with Heidi Sioux's groom. She had learned that the grooms, who were constantly around the horses, could often tell you more than the trainers about the condition of a horse.

"How's she feeling today?" she asked the groom who was brushing the mare's glossy coat.

"Ready to go," he said. "Bardy never hired no girl jockeys before."

Sabina had stopped taking offense at most of

these remarks years before. The prejudice was so rampant, you could drive yourself crazy being on the bandstand all the time. "Yeah," she said with a smile. "I guess I got lucky."

The groom chuckled as he used a hoof pick. "It ain't luck, lady. A powerful friend is what you got. Not many trainers out here who would turn down a request from Miguel Carrasco."

She looked at him with surprise. "You mean Carrasco called Mulligan and asked him to put me on this horse?"

"You didn't know that?" He looked at her suspiciously.

She shook her head. "Honestly, I didn't."

"Yeah, well, Carrasco called yesterday afternoon. I know, 'cause I was in the office when he called. Bardy says, yeah, you're a pretty good rider, but he don't want to give you no horse. Says the owners would get jittery about a girl out there. I don't know what Carrasco says to him, but when Bardy hung up the phone, you got a horse that Carrasco was scheduled to ride today."

As Sabina walked back to the jockey room to change for the race, she marveled at what Miguel had done. No wonder he hadn't seemed surprised that she'd gotten the mount. He would have been surprised if she hadn't.

Bardy Mulligan was a meticulous horseman. While they were in the paddock area just before the race, he double-checked much of what the groom had done. He even lifted each of the horse's hooves, and with a hoof pick, cleaned one out. Then he tucked the horse's forelock under the bridle. In the walking ring he gave Sabina some last-minute instructions before giving her a leg up.

As she paraded past the stands Paul McDonald came up alongside her. "Miguel called me this morning and told me to remind you to put your goggles down."

"Good advice," she said with a laugh.

"And he warned me that if I dared shut you off, he'd break both my legs. So I guess I'll keep out of your way."

"He really threatened to break both your legs?"

"Nah. That's an exaggeration. Only one of my legs. Miguel's not excessive. You going to pull ahead of me today?"

"You bet." If she'd ever been on a horse that had the potential to beat an odds-on favorite, today was the day. Bardy had not been enthusiastic about Heidi Sioux, but Sabina had checked out her record, and although she had not placed in her most recent race, her last workout indicated she was in excellent shape.

Once loaded into the gate Sabina positioned Heidi Sioux against the back so that when breaking out, she would spring off it and not take a step backward before moving out. Those few lost seconds could be precious for a horse that needed to be in front.

After putting down her goggles she took a grip on the horse's mane and relaxed, waiting for the flag to go up. Staying relaxed in the starting gate had been one of the hardest things to learn when she'd been an apprentice jockey, as the natural tendency was to tense up in readiness. But a racehorse was quick to react to the slightest

change in a rider's body, and the wisest thing a
jockey could do at that point was to keep the
horse calm.

She was expecting a fast break, but Heidi Sioux
flew out of the gate with such lightning speed that
it took Sabina pleasantly by surprise. She was
thrilled to find herself a full length in front of the
entire field of horses. Never in her life had she
been on a horse out of the gate faster.

Heidi Sioux set the pace for the rest of the
horses, and while letting her stay out front,
Sabina tried to keep her in an easy stride so she'd
still have the stamina for the final stretch run.

Around the turn the pace quickened when the
others began moving up, but Heidi Sioux was not
giving up her position. Eventually Sabina might
have to go to the whip, but not now. Heidi Sioux
was moving onto the bit, pushing ahead on her
own.

Into the stretch she looked under her arm and
saw a horse coming up alongside her. She un-
cocked her stick.

They were in the closing yards. Sabina sensed
the horse had the energy, but nothing she did
could get Heidi Sioux to pull ahead.

The other horse was tiring badly, straining to
keep with the pace. But amazingly the jockey was
not going to the whip. As they crossed the finish
line they were nose and nose. She might have it,
but it was too close to call.

Sabina saluted the stewards and waited nervously in front of the grandstands for the results.
Her heart sank when she saw the number go up
on the tote board.

Logically she knew that second place wasn't

bad, but damn! She'd had the horse this time. She should have won it.

Worst of all, she felt that she'd let Miguel down. He had put himself out to get her the best horse of her life, and somehow she had blown it.

That was the first thing she said when he greeted her at his door that night.

"Did you bring the tape of the race?" he asked her.

She nodded. "I played it over and over in the jockey's room after the race. I don't know what I could have done differently."

"Did she have trouble with her leads?"

"Not a bit. She was perfect—and fitter than any horse on the track. She stayed out in front, even when the others were trying to force the pace. Lopez's horse was fading; I could see it. I should have won."

"We'll take a look after dinner and see. But from what I heard, you nearly did win."

"Nearly isn't good enough," she said with a sigh. "That horse had more going for her than any of them. I've never seen anything like the way she broke out of the gate. It was as though she had sprouted wings."

"She is quick out of the gate," he agreed. "Don't be so hard on yourself. That was your first time on her. Next time you'll win it."

"If Bardy gives me another chance to ride."

"He will. I spoke to him. He was pleased with your ride."

As they walked into his living room, she said hesitantly, "Miguel, I know that you called him. I appreciate it, but . . ."

"But what?"

"Oh, I don't know. I just feel a little funny about it, that's all."

He took her hand between his. "Sabina, it is not the first time I've called a trainer about a rider I thought should be given a chance on a good horse. And it won't be the last. I'm sure you've done it, too."

That was true. There had been many times in the Midwest, when she had been winning regularly for a trainer, that she'd applied some pressure to get a mount for a friend who had some ability.

They sat down on a couch that faced an immense fireplace. A crackling blaze warmed her, dispelling the cold dampness she had brought in with her from outside.

They were in a large living room with the same inlaid parquet floors as the foyer. Much of the furniture was antique, and the numerous paintings and engravings, as in the rest of the house, were of Miguel's favorite subject. Over the mantelpiece was a magnificent portrait of a black racehorse. Curious about the painting's position of honor, she asked about it.

Miguel leaned back on the couch and gazed up at the painting. "She was a beauty, a filly named Cocoletta. I won my first race in this country on her, and many others. She, too, was quick out of the gate, and an affectionate horse, so kind and gentle you could probably have put a child on her. I have always had a soft spot in my heart for that horse.

"After they retired her, she went off her feed and started to lose weight. Nobody could figure out what was wrong with her. Finally somebody had the inspiration to bring her back to the track. As soon as that mare heard the hornblower play the "First Call," she perked up her ears and was fine. For some horses, just like people, the track is life."

"I'll probably be like that," mused Sabina. "When I'm too old to race, I'll try to be a trainer, and if I'm not any good at that, I'll sell Racing Forms at the gate, anything to stay at the track."

Miguel laughed. "Somehow I can't see you content with selling Racing Forms."

"What were the results of the X-rays today?"

He frowned. "As usual. They show that I've broken a number of bones."

"What did Dr. Backer say?"

"That I should stop racing."

"What would you do then?"

"Stop breathing."

"There you are getting morbid again. Really, Miguel, what will you do? You must have thought about it."

He gazed back up at the portrait of Cocoletta. "I think you had the right idea."

"Become a trainer?"

"No. The other idea. Perhaps one day you and I will be standing at the gate competing to see who can sell the most Racing Forms."

"I take it you have decided to ignore Dr. Backer again."

"He is worried I will break some more bones. That doesn't bother me. I'll keep racing."

They dined at one end of a table that could have seated twenty people comfortably. It was set with elegant china, silver and crystal a maharaja would not have been loathe to use. Indeed, it made the elegant picnic-wear look like paper cups and plates.

Never having had servants, Sabina was fascinated by the way Miguel handled the maid and butler who served them. It reminded her of the ease with which he handled a thoroughbred. In a quiet way he was firmly in control. That kind of gentility was inbred, she thought.

And yet, there was also a streak of wildness just below the polished surface, like the scarcely controlled violence of a well-schooled stallion that had been turned loose on the range for a year, then brought back to civilization. Miguel could joke about breaking someone's legs, but there was something in his dark eyes that told her if he were ever really provoked, he was perfectly capable of it.

After dinner they went into his library, a richly paneled room filled with volumes in Spanish and English. If his formal education had been interrupted, his informal one had not.

He slid the videotape of the race into his recorder, and they sat down on a brown leather couch to watch.

"Ah," he said as he watched her and Lopez coming into the stretch. "He's a clever son-of-bitch," said Miguel with a laugh. "Do you see what he's doing with his stick?"

"Nothing. That's what amazed me. His horse was dog tired, but he didn't even go to the stick. And still he was keeping right up there with me."

"He wasn't keeping up with you. He was keeping you from passing him."

"Impossible."

He ran the tape again. "Look at the way he is

holding that stick." It was something Sabina hadn't noticed during the race. Usually a jockey held his whip straight down, but there was nothing illegal in what he was doing. "He probably wasn't thinking about it," said Sabina.

"Lopez? Not likely. He never stops thinking out there on the track. He's one of the smartest jockeys I've ever met. He knew damn well that if he held the stick out there in front of Heidi Sioux's eye, she wouldn't pass it. Few horses would. Now, look how he handles it right as you go under the wire."

She saw him bring the whip forward and flick it beside his horse's eye.

"It's a good trick," said Miguel, "when you're that close. It made the mare lift her head just enough for him to win by a nose."

She shook her head. "That kind of thing is so subtle compared to what I'm used to! On some of the smaller tracks without cameras to catch things, guys used to pull all kinds of dirty tricks. They'd grab your saddle cloth or your reins. I even had a guy slap me across the back with a whip once when I came up beside him."

Miguel's eyes grew black with an expression she thought he'd use before he broke someone's legs. "What did you do about it?"

"That time I reported it. He claimed I was lying, but I had the welts to prove it. Most of the time I just let it go. That's just the way things are at those tracks. But you can see why I'd like to stay at San Felipe."

He was shocked that jockeys would be so rough with a woman rider.

"They're out there to win their percentage of

the purse money. It wouldn't matter if I were the Princess of Wales out there."

He reset the video recorder. "All right, princess. We know why you lost in the last seconds. Let's see what you did before." He played her cassette over again, stopping the tape, putting it in slow motion, analyzing in detail all of her moves and the moves of other riders. By the time he was through, she had received one of the most helpful critiques of her life.

"Do you have a tape player at home?" he asked her.

She was barely meeting her car payments. "No, but I always see the replays in the jockey's room."

"That's not enough. You should be analyzing everything. At a track like San Felipe you need all the aids you can get. Before your next race we'll go through my tape library. I will tell you about each of the riders, and what kind of tricks or strategy they are likely to use in a given situation. With some of them you cannot tell. They will wait until they are on the track and see what needs to be done. That is the way I like to ride. But many are predictable, as are some of the horses. Right now you're a very good rider; you could be one of the best, maybe even one of the greats. But you make small mistakes. In the Midwest you were good enough to get away with it, but the guys who ride at San Felipe don't make mistakes. If you are willing to learn, I'll help you."

She was moved by what he said. "It's really kind of you to take all this time with me, Miguel. I do appreciate it."

"I've got more time than I know what to do

with right now, waiting for the ankle to get in shape. You would be doing me a favor."

"How is your ankle tonight?"

"Much better, thank you."

"And Natasha?"

"That is painful."

"You don't love her anymore?"

Miguel cupped her small face in the palm of his large hand and rubbed a thumb across her cheek. "You didn't like the way I was treating her the other night, did you?"

"We're friends, so I'll be honest with you. I thought you were callous to flirt with me. I could see she was suffering."

"That's why I decided I liked you," he said. "Most women would not have cared about Natasha's feelings."

"You certainly didn't."

"But, you are wrong," he said. "I care very deeply about her feelings. But she had to realize that it is finished between us."

Sabina gave him an accusing look. "And that's another thing I didn't like, your using me like that. If you wanted to end things with her, at least be out front and say, 'Hey, look, Natasha, it's over.'"

"I did, only I must say I phrased it a little more gently than that."

"If you had ended it more forcefully, she might not have gotten the wrong idea. This way she probably thinks you still care about her."

"I do."

"Then why did you break up with her?"

"Because I could not give her what she wants."

"And that is . . . ?"

"A life. Natasha is a fine dancer, but she is getting past the age where she can perform as well as she used to. She would like to retire, get married and have children."

"And you didn't love her enough for that?"

"I did love her. But I am like you, Sabina. There is only one thing in my life that really matters."

"But when the day comes where you're standing at the gate with me selling Racing Forms, wouldn't it be nice to trudge home each night to a wife and kids all lined up at the front door in matching ballet leotards?"

He threw his head back and laughed. "Matching leotards?"

"All right, so maybe the kids will take after you and all be lined up in matching racing silks with Caliente helmets on their precious little heads."

"I'll have to sell a lot of Racing Forms to keep them in racing silks," he mused.

"Sure, but think about the trend you could set. Once the fad caught on, you'd send the designer-jean people into bankruptcy."

Sabina suddenly yawned. "Late nights were made for people who don't have to get up at five," she apologized. "I guess I'd better be going before I do something really gauche like fall asleep on you."

"You are welcome to stay here if you don't want to drive all the way home," he offered.

She couldn't help thinking of the beautiful bedroom with the fireplace.

Reading her mind, he quickly added. "In a guest room, of course. Unless you have changed your mind about our becoming friends. . . ." He reached over and ran his hand down her arm. It made her tremble. She stood up abruptly before she could change her mind.

"I don't live that far," she said.

He looked up at her and laughed. "It is hard to believe that the same girl I just saw on tape, slamming that horse across the finish line, would be so terrified of a love affair. I still think you are not telling me all there is to know about Frank."

She glared at him angrily. "There is nothing between me and Frank except a few racehorses."

He shut one eye and scrutinized her. She could tell he was still unconvinced. He reached for her hand and pulled her back down on the couch beside him.

"There is one thing I demand from my friends, Sabina, and that is honesty."

"I don't know why this is so important to you," she said with a weary sigh.

There was a dark intensity in his eyes that was almost frightening. "Honesty is the most important thing between two people. That is something that was impressed upon me as a child. It was my father's best friend who betrayed him. If a person lies to me once and I learn of it, that is the end of the friendship. No going back."

"I'm not lying to you, Miguel," she said softly. "And I feel the same way about friends." She touched his cheek, tracing the rough-edged line of his jaw.

The color in his dark eyes changed as he gazed at her. It became a deep, velvety black. His hand went around the back of her neck, drawing her face to his.

The touch of his lips sent shivers through her body. Her hands slipped around his back as he lowered her onto the couch.

No. She didn't really want this. It was too soon . . . too soon. . . .

But her mouth was opening to his, welcoming, beckoning, even teasing. Her breasts slid against the hardness of his chest. His mouth was moving down her neck as he brushed her long hair aside. Deft fingers were unbuttoning her blouse. The material parted. His mouth was on her breasts and her back was arching to receive his kisses, the tantalizing flicks of his tongue on the satin tips of her breasts.

"Oh, Miguel. . . ."

His legs were between hers, forcing them open. She felt the pressure of his body and wanted it, wanted him to love her. Soon, she would forget . . . forget. This would make her forget. Miguel would make her forget.

Al's face came back to her, and she pushed it from her mind. Like the race. She couldn't look back. Too painful to look back. And nothing she could do to help.

Miguel's hand was caressing one breast, his mouth the other. Erotic waves enveloped her, wrapping silken ribbons around the lower half of her body.

"Sabina, I've wanted you for so long," he murmured against her mouth. His hand was now where his hard thigh had been, exploring, rubbing. Her own thighs pushed against his hand, gripping as though they were the hard flanks of a horse.

The need in her was violent, and Miguel felt it. His breathing was ragged as he unhooked her slacks and pulled on the zipper.

"Oh . . ." His hand slid down over the smoothness of her belly. Her head twisted from side to side. Something told her to stop him now before it was too late. Was it already too late?

He was sliding the slacks over her knees, and she was doing nothing to stop him. He was kissing the soft skin of her inner thighs, nibbling gently. She felt the roughness of his cheeks against her.

Strong, powerful hands were stroking from her breasts to her rib cage and down over her hips. He used long, sweeping motions, willing her to give everything.

Miguel removed his shirt and threw it to the floor, and she ran her fingers through the dark, coarse chest hair.

Then suddenly it was there again. The vision of Al. Al had been the only one. And now . . .

Her fingers fumbled with Miguel's belt buckle. He started to help her, but then she shook her head. "No." Her fingers were trembling. She made them into fists and closed her eyes tightly to keep back the tears.

"Sabina, what is it?" His voice was hoarse.

"Can't," she said. "I can't. . . ."

His hands were on her shoulders, gripping tightly. "Tell me, Sabina."

"I can't make love to you," she blurted out.

"If you're worried about protection. . . ."

He was giving her an easy out. An easy lie. But she had promised not to lie to him. "No," she said, "that's not a problem."

"Then what is it?"

He was sitting beside her, and she curled her body around him while he stroked her hair.

He changed his question. "Who is it, Sabina?"

She shook her head. It was as though Al were there in the room with them. She did not want to mention his name. One day she would tell Miguel, but not tonight.

"Miguel . . . can we be friends? Is it too late? I just . . . I need a friend. Please. . . ."

"Of course, *amigita*." His voice was low and soothing, though she could sense the restraint. She had taken him past the starting gate and then refused to let him finish the race.

It had been futile to think she could forget so easily. In spite of all that she was beginning to feel for Miguel, it would take much longer to put Al's death behind her.

Perhaps Miguel was the wrong one to make her forget. He had made it clear by what he'd said about Natasha that he didn't want any enduring involvements. Racing was the only thing that mattered to him. That was the way it should be for her, too.

All of a sudden she had a strange vision of a group of little jockey-clad children, hers and Miguel's. Why such a thought would pop into her head at that minute, she didn't know.

"Are you all right now?" he asked.

She nodded. "I'm sorry . . . about this. It wasn't fair to you."

"Or you," he said softly. "Let's talk."

"Not now. I'd better go home."

"How about breakfast tomorrow at the track?"

"Yes. I'd like that."

He walked her out to the car and locked the car door before he shut it. "Drive safely."

She forced a smile. Her fingers were still shaking as she turned the key in the ignition.

"Sabina, call me when you get home so I'll know you're all right."

She nodded and put the car in gear.

The moment she stepped into her apartment, she dialed his number. He sounded relieved to hear her voice.

She tried to make a joke. "You showed more concern about my getting home than my getting a horse around the track."

"Don't kid yourself, *amigita.*"

Chapter 5

SHE WORKED HORSES AGAIN FOR BARDY MULLIGAN
the next morning, and as Miguel had predicted,
he asked her to ride two more horses the following week. She was still no Paul McDonald or
Miguel Carrasco, who rode horses in almost every
race, five days a week, but the horses were from
Bardy Mulligan's barn, and that in itself was an
improvement over riding for Frank Lathrop.

As she finished galloping Xenophon again, she
saw Miguel standing by the rail, watching her.
"Hola, amigita!" he called to her.

She felt her pulse take off. This is crazy, she
thought to herself as she connected with the pony
rider. I'm falling for him whether I want to or not.

They had breakfast outside in the restaurant at
Clocker's Corner, just below where the officials
timed horses around the track.

Several people stopped by the table to ask

Miguel when he would be riding again. "As soon as the swelling in my ankle is down," he answered.

"You're very nice to your fans," she complimented him, after several had stopped to ask for autographs.

"Fans can turn on you when they have money on your horse and you lose, but most of them are nice people."

A balding, elderly man with a red carnation boutonniere, made his way cautiously to the table, looked around to see if anyone was within earshot and asked Miguel in a low voice, "What do you think of Marvelous Marv in the third race?"

"He might run some," said Miguel just above a whisper.

The man grinned, thanked him profusely for the advice and walked off.

Sabina glanced down at the racing program in front of her. "Miguel, there is no Marvelous Marv entered in the third race."

"I know. He asks me the same thing every day," confided Miguel. "Same horse, same race. There is no Marvelous Marv in any race, for that matter. Out of curiosity I checked into it once. The horse used to run in Florida in the thirties."

"Was the horse any good?"

Miguel laughed. "Not bad."

As they discussed some of the horses that were on the program for that afternoon, Paul McDonald stopped by the table.

"How's Chloe?" asked Miguel.

"Still sniffling, but her spirits are much improved, especially after that little gift you sent her. Miguel, you're going to spoil some poor kid one day."

"He sent Chloe the video cassette of *Mary Poppins*," Paul explained to Sabina. "And now Janice and I have to suffer through it three times a day. The least you could do, Carrasco, is come over and sit through it with us. What are you doing for dinner tonight?"

Miguel shrugged.

"Good. Then, you're on. How about you, Sabina? How do you feel about Mary Poppins?"

"I love the movie," she said with a laugh. "And I'd love to join you, but I'm going over to my parents house tonight for dinner. Some other time I'd be glad to."

"I'll hold you to that," promised Paul as he walked back down the stairs toward the barns.

Just as they were finishing breakfast Sabina saw Patsy Dimpton heading toward them. That morning it had seemed that she couldn't turn around, especially at Bardy's barn, without seeing those bright eyes. Patsy was full of questions about racing, but it seemed to Sabina that the girl was more interested in wedging her way into Bardy Mulligan's consciousness than in gleaning any jewels of information.

"Hi, guys."

Miguel flashed her a friendly smile. "Pardon me, but I don't believe we have met."

"I'm Patsy Dimpton." She extended her hand. "I'm an exercise girl. Sabina and I are real good friends."

Sabina nearly choked on her coffee. Both statements were doubtful.

"Then won't you sit down and join us?" Miguel stood up politely and offered her a chair.

"That would be super." Not waiting for a second invitation from Sabina, Patsy sat down quickly and gazed up flirtatiously at Miguel. "Do you know that I have idolized you for years?"

Sabina's English muffin suddenly tasted like cardboard.

"Do you want to be a jockey like Sabina?" asked Miguel.

"Oh, no." Patsy displayed her dimples. "I want to be a jockey like you."

Amazingly, Miguel seemed to be charmed and more than politely interested. Was it that Patsy, with her tiny frame and ash-blond hair, looked something like Natasha? Was he, heaven forbid, finding her equally as attractive?

Miguel and I are only friends, she reminded herself. I have no right to be jealous. And yet the gnawing feeling continued as Patsy confided her innermost ambitions to Miguel.

Before, Sabina had been slightly irritated and vaguely amused by Patsy Dimpton. Now, as hard as she tried to rise above the baseness of her feelings, Sabina began to feel the seeds of irrational loathing implanting themselves as she watched Patsy touch Miguel's hand and consciously display her bosom as she leaned over the table.

Frank had probably been right after all. Patsy was eighteen going on fifty. She knew exactly where she wanted to go and how she was going to get there. If it took spending a few minutes on her back to get a horse to exercise, she'd do it without blinking an innocent blue eye. No doubt she had learned through the track grapevine that Miguel Carrasco had been instrumental in getting her Heidi Sioux to ride yesterday. That would put him at the top of Patsy's list of possible conquests.

Suddenly Sabina looked up and saw Frank Lathrop walking onto the patio. He was alone and about to take a nearby table. After watching Patsy in action, Sabina realized her feelings of disgust for Frank had considerably mellowed. Patsy had probably profited more from the arrangement than he had.

She noticed Patsy look from Frank to Miguel in a calculated assessment of where her best interests lay.

Trying to figure out where Patsy was going to focus her attention was a little like handicapping a race. Frank, being alone, was the odds-on favorite. He had proven his worth by giving her exercise mounts. Miguel Carrasco might be a longshot, in that he was better looking and harder to get, but a man who wielded that kind of power was not to be scoffed at. And he definitely gave every appearance of being interested.

A rather perverse scheme materialized in the dark regions of Sabina's brain, and before she could think it over, she acted.

"Hi, Frank," she called out. "Why don't you join us?"

Everyone, including Frank, looked surprised at her friendly invitation.

"No sense eating alone," she repeated, careful not to let a trace of sarcasm pass her lips.

"Uh, I was just going to have a cup of coffee,"

he said uncomfortably, shifting his weight from one foot to the other.

"No reason you can't have it here," she said pleasantly. Her tone was so friendly and sincere that he had no choice but to take her up on the offer.

Patsy twisted a spoon nervously. This would be a tough decision. Sabina was enjoying the other girl's discomfort immensely.

"Do you exercise horses for Frank?" Miguel asked Patsy.

"Yes," she said brightly. "In fact, Frank was the very first trainer to give me a horse. I just got my license the other day."

"That was good of you," Miguel said cautiously.

"Uh, yeah. Patsy does all right." His face flushed slightly, and he pretended to watch the action of some horses out on the track.

"Did you guys know that Sabina is going to hold a class and help a bunch of us girls who want to be jockeys?"

"That's very generous of you, Sabina, but you must be careful about helping the competition. One afternoon you could be looking over your shoulder and find Patsy gaining on you."

"I guess that's a chance I'll have to take," she said with a shrug.

Frank was still not sure what to make of the situation and shifted nervously in his chair. "When are you going to be racing again?" he asked Miguel.

"I'll be back soon."

A waitress came to take orders from the new

arrivals, but both Patsy and Frank declined anything.

Frank stood up. "If you folks will excuse me, I just remembered a phone call I have to make. Uh, hope your ankle's better," he said to Miguel. Then to Patsy and Sabina he added, "See you girls around."

Patsy excused herself a few minutes after Frank left, exclaiming profusely about how honored she was to have met a living legend. Miguel accepted it all graciously. As he walked her back to the parking area Sabina noticed a change in his mood, a certain tenseness about him.

"Interesting little scene you orchestrated back there with Frank and Patsy."

She smiled. "I thought so."

For some reason he wasn't taking it lightly.

"Miguel, you're angry," she said with surprise.

"Disappointed."

"That I brought Frank over to the table with Patsy? I admit, it was a little perverse on my part, but nobody was hurt. They were a little shaken up, maybe, but not hurt."

His lips were set in a grim line. "So Patsy was the source of your argument with Frank."

"No, it had been coming on for a long time. She was just the proverbial straw that broke the camel's back."

"So Patsy wasn't the only one you had to share him with?"

"What?"

"I've never seen a man look more guilty than Frank Lathrop did a few minutes ago. It was an inspired bit of staging, Sabina."

"Oh, Lord, Miguel. You've got it all twisted! I didn't lie to you. Believe me, Frank and I weren't even dating. He did get involved with Patsy, though, and I gave him a bad time about it."

"Why would that matter to you if you weren't involved with him?" asked Miguel suspiciously.

"Because . . . well . . ." Sabina didn't want to go into the whole story. What Patsy and Frank did was really their business. And if that was the way Patsy found horses to ride, that was her business, too.

"Well?"

Sabina sighed. "Just take my word for it, Miguel. Frank Lathrop means nothing to me. Our arguments stemmed from the way he was treating me in front of the owners."

He gazed at her for a long moment, and she could see the taut muscle in his neck relax. He slipped an arm around her shoulders and kissed her on the cheek. "Sabina, *amigita,* what Frank is or was to you is not the point. Understand that. I thought you had not been telling me the truth. Don't ever feel you have to lie to me. Ever."

Sabina felt the warmth of that statement fill her. It was good to know that he cared enough for her to want that.

"Please trust me," she said softly.

"I will. Have a good dinner tonight."

For a brief moment she wanted to invite him along, even though he had already committed himself to Paul and Janice's. Her father, who had once wanted to be a jockey, was an enthusiastic Miguel Carrasco fan. It would be a thrill for him to meet the famous jockey. But her mother—that was another story. Sabina couldn't bring another jockey home. Not after what she'd told her mother about Al.

Miguel would not have approved of the lie she had told her mother. But it had been necessary. Some lies were necessary, no matter what Miguel thought.

The first message on her answering machine was from her mother. "Honey, we have to cancel out tonight. Dad had to fly up to San Francisco for some location shooting and decided to take me along. We're going to stay a few days. Call you when we get back. Take care, darling."

Her first thought was to call Miguel and go with him to Paul and Janice's. But as she picked up the phone to dial his number, she remembered the scene the night before on his couch. Things were moving far too quickly with him, and she wasn't sure she'd have the willpower to stop him again. She needed a breather to sort things out.

She checked her other messages. Her agent had called to confirm her mounts on Bardy's horses. There was another trainer who also had a horse he wanted her to ride the following week. She was to stop by his barn tomorrow. "Things are picking up a little for you, at least," her agent said.

The other message, she was surprised to learn, was from Frank Lathrop. It was terse. "Sabina, just call me when you get in. I'll be at the track."

Too intrigued not to call, she dialed the familiar number. One of the grooms answered and after a moment she heard Frank's voice.

"I've been thinking a lot about what you said

the other day. That business with Patsy, especially. I guess I started thinking about my daughter and—" he paused to clear his throat "—and I probably shouldn't have spoken to you that way. You've done a good job with my horses, especially Gusty. Nobody thought he was worth anything until you started riding him. I guess what I'm trying to say is that I want to apologize."

Sabina hit the side of her head a few times to make sure she had heard him correctly. Frank Lathrop was actually apologizing to her? She had orchestrated her little scene that morning for entirely different purposes, but that magnanimous "Let bygones be bygones" pose had served to clear the air between them.

"I apologize, too, for flying off the handle," she said. "I'm glad we've straightened that out."

"Uh, listen, Sabina. I don't know if you're free tonight, but my daughter's home from college for spring break. You met her when I brought her to the track last Christmas. Well, she's become kind of a fan of yours. I'm going to take her out to a nice dinner tonight. She'd sure get a kick out of it if you'd like to join us."

He really was trying to make it up to her. Sabina was touched. "Sure, I'd love to. She was studying computer science, wasn't she?"

"Yes. She's got my ex-wife's brains, not mine. Unfortunately she's inherited my temper. How about if we pick you up around six? I know you don't like to stay out late, and she's got some rock concert she's going to later."

"Sounds fine," said Sabina, and hung up the phone in wonderment at the human race. The next time someone argued that criminals couldn't be rehabilitated, she would think of Frank Lathrop.

Being around his daughter seemed to bring out the best in Frank, thought Sabina as they walked into the French restaurant, La Chambre Bleu. It was perhaps the most expensive restaurant in San Felipe, and seeing Frank, the perennial tightwad, ready to spend that much money was a revelation. His daughter meant a lot to him. Comparing Patsy to her had probably affected him even more than she'd imagined.

Sabina could sense his disappointment that Lisa, with the thoughtless self-interest of youth, was not planning to spend the entire evening with her father. She had made a date with a student she'd met on the plane who had tickets to a rock concert at the Forum. He would pick her up at the restaurant.

They had a pleasant dinner, and just before desert the young man arrived in a great hurry to get to the concert. Much to Frank's relief the kid looked very clean-cut and collegiate and called him sir.

As Sabina watched them go she wondered if she might have missed out on an important phase of her youth. She really wasn't too much older than Lisa. Her parents had always wanted her to go to college, but she was headstrong. Horse racing was all she'd wanted to do, and she'd begun her career the day after she graduated from high school.

There had never been time for rock concerts or wild partying. It was a gypsy existence, going from track to track. Al had been her social life, and aside from a movie now and then they had gone out rarely. Their lives were centered around racing, and their excitement came from the unpredictability of their risky profession.

As she was musing about this to Frank over strawberries covered with a delicious Grand Marnier sauce, he suddenly glanced toward the entrance. "Oh, there's your friend Carrasco."

Sabina's heart stopped as she turned her head slowly. Miguel was with Paul and Janice and holding the hand of a little girl about seven years old.

"Fancy meeting you here," said Janice, wending her way to their table. "Don't tell me horse people don't know the best places to eat."

The little girl, who was keeping a tight grasp on Miguel's hand, was introduced as Paul and Janice's daughter, Chloe, who had staged such a miraculous recovery from the sniffles that Miguel was taking them all out to celebrate the event.

"I'm Miguel's date tonight," the little girl informed them possessively. He enthralled them at any age, Sabina mused, but there was something utterly appealing about seeing him with that child. It was obvious the adoration was mutual. The thought of miniature jockeys in racing silks popped once again into her head. He would make some child a wonderful father.

But Miguel was looking anything but the picture of paternal affection. He was glaring at Sabina with angry intensity. She realized what he was thinking. Her apparent tête-à-tête with Frank would confirm what he had suspected all along.

"My daughter was home from college for

spring break," said Frank. "So I wanted to take her someplace classy for dinner. She just left a few minutes ago to go to a punk rock concert." If Sabina thought that the mention of Lisa would prove her innocence, she was wrong. Miguel continued to shoot visual daggers at her.

She made a silent plea with her eyes, begging him not to think the worst, but it did not change his hard, uncompromising expression.

Unable to communicate with him, she tried to wrench her gaze away from his, but he held it.

"Well, nice seeing you, folks," said Paul, turning back to their table.

"Yeah, see you all tomorrow at the track," said Frank.

Neither Sabina nor Miguel spoke, and he was not moving.

Little Chloe began yanking impatiently on Miguel's hand. "Are we really going to eat a chocolate moose?" she asked.

Miguel smiled down at her, his expression changing quickly to one of warmth. "Chocolate mousse," he said. "It's like a big fluffy pudding. It's so big that you will never be able to finish it. Not in a hundred million billion years."

"I will so," protested Chloe with a giggle and an irresistible little girl squirm.

Sabina's heart turned over.

Briefly he focused his attention back on Sabina, his dark eyes holding hers captive for a moment more; then he released her and walked to his table.

"Not a bad friend for you to have, Sabina," said Frank.

"Yes, he is." The strawberries no longer looked

appealing, but she rearranged them with her spoon to have something to do.

"I've got to admit, I didn't think you were going to have an easy time of it when you walked away from my barn the other day. But you did all right for yourself."

There was no malice or sarcasm in Frank's voice. He was talking practicality.

"It's not what you think," she said quietly. "I'm not having an affair with him."

"Did I say you were?" He was anxious to avoid a fight. "I just said you were lucky to have him as a friend. Not many guys would stick their necks out to get you one of Mulligan's horses. But you did pretty well with that mare. I figured you would. In fact, if the truth be known, I put a hundred dollars on you to place." He chuckled self-consciously. "You might say you're paying for this dinner. Thanks to your friend over there."

Sabina couldn't help laughing. "Well, that's all Carrasco is, a friend." Though at the moment she wasn't even sure if he was still that.

"From the tone of your voice, it sounds like that doesn't quite suit you."

"No. Suits me fine."

"And the way you looked at him. . . ."

"How about if we talk about something else, Frank?"

"Kind of touchy, aren't you?" He was enjoying her discomfort. Some of the old Frank seeping through. You couldn't entirely rehabilitate a criminal.

"Was Gusty sore after the last race?" she asked to change the subject.

"Not too bad. You will ride him again for me, won't you?"

"You know I like that horse."

He threw an arm around her shoulders and gave her a kiss on the cheek. "You liked that horse better'n you liked me."

She stole a glance in Miguel's direction. He had seen the kiss and hug. Things couldn't get much worse. She was relieved when the check came.

As they left they stopped by Miguel's table briefly, and she kept her eyes averted from his. By this time Janice and Paul had noticed the strain, but there was nothing anyone could say.

Back home, inside her apartment, she sank down into her blue garage-sale armchair.

The seat cushion turned up on the ends, and for some uncanny reason it seemed to be smiling at her. Traveling from track to track, she had never bothered to accumulate furniture. And she would not have begun now, except that it had been impossible to pass up a chair that smiled so beguilingly at her.

The woman running the sale had been asking ten dollars, and Sabina had shrewdly bargained her down to five. The chair probably hadn't been worth half that, but it had more than paid for itself in her opinion. There had been many a night when, sore from work, she'd been grateful to have that smile to sink into. Tonight was one of them.

It was a night when she felt like opening her scrapbooks one by one and looking through her life as an outsider might. There were the child-hood snapshots: pictures of her dressed up as a cowgirl on her first horse, a small dapple-gray Arabian. He was a fast little horse, she remembered. Even then she used to win races with her friends in the park. Then there was the horse show era as a teenager: photos of her in jodhpurs jumping horses. She had saved all the armbands with numbers from horseshows she'd won.

And the racing pictures, the photos from the winning circles. In some of them she was smiling; in others she looked a little dazed. She even had some of the programs from those winning races, the newspaper clippings. A national women's magazine had once done an article on women jockeys, and she'd been included as one of the top riders in the country. They'd had a professional makeup artist and hairstylist for her out at the track that day, and although the photos were very glamorous, she didn't think they looked much like her.

There were pictures of her and Al clowning around at various racetracks. There he was squinting into the sun with his boyish, lopsided grin—so unlike Miguel's roguish smile, with its glint of white teeth, which turned her heart upside down.

But the photos of Al were few in comparison to the photos of horses. She had loved him, but the story she read in the scrapbooks was clearly one of a woman's ongoing obsession with fast, four-legged animals.

The telephone rang. She picked it up hoping it was Miguel, but it was Charlotte Ficus.

"How're you doing?"

"Wonderful," Sabina answered without enthusiasm. Charlotte was the last person to whom she'd reveal the real state of her mind. "How are you, Charlotte?"

"Never felt better." Charlotte had the annoyingly cheery sound of an energetic high school athletic coach. "Hey, you ready for this? Guess who we've got an appointment with tomorrow at noon?"

"Who?" She'd play along.

"Bob Perile! Isn't that great?"

"Terrific." She tried to work a little excitement into the response.

"Now, be sure to wear something smart so we go in there looking like we know what we're doing. Let's meet at clockers' corner beforehand to discuss our strategy. Say, about eleven forty-five."

"Marvelous," said Sabina, hoping the conversation would end soon. She was running out of superlatives with which to respond. Why did some people always elicit superlative responses?

After she hung up, she began thinking about the possibility of an all-women race. There were a lot of friends she'd made over the years who were doing fairly well in different parts of the country. What fun it would be to bring them all together. It was a group of gutsy individuals. Would staid San Felipe be ready for the powerhouse those women would represent?

She looked at the telephone again. Miguel would probably be home by now. They wouldn't keep Chloe out late.

She dialed his number. Whether he believed her or not, she had to try to explain. Wasn't it

against the law to convict someone on circumstan-
tial evidence?

The maid answered. "No, Mr. Carrasco is not
at home. Would you care to leave a message?"

"Yes, I would. Please tell him that . . . uh no,
on second thought. Thanks, anyway, I'll call back
later."

But she wouldn't. She didn't want to explain
over the phone. She had to see him face to face.

Chapter 6

SABINA LOOKED FOR MIGUEL AT CLOCKERS' CORNER when she took her break at eight the next morning, but he was not there. Patsy, bubbling with excitement, was, however.

"That Miguel Carrasco is soooo darling. I saw him around here earlier and he bought me a cup of coffee. Those *eyes* of his."

Sabina was once again in the grip of the green-eyed monster. "Mmm, he is good-looking," she mumbled.

"Listen, Sabina, are you dating him or anything?"

Sabina was not feeling kind. "Would that make a difference to you?"

Patsy turned a shade of pink. "Listen, Sabina, I didn't go out with Frank to get at you or anything. That was strictly business. You've been really decent to me, and I'm not about to screw things up for you. If you tell me Carrasco is off-limits, I'll keep away from him."

The way Patsy had been flirting with him, Sabina hardly thought this was the time to be asking permission. It was like closing the barn door after the horse had run away.

And what could she say? She had no claim to Miguel. She had told him she just wanted to be friends, and now that he'd seen her out with Frank, she was sure he was no longer interested in her. Patsy had as much right to him as anyone. "You figure Miguel could do you more good than Frank?" Sabina asked.

"Look what he's done for you," said Patsy logically. "There are jockeys who would shoot their own mothers for a chance to ride Mulligan's horses."

Maybe Patsy was exactly the sort of woman Miguel should have. No danger of confusing her emotions. Patsy would simply use him to further her career and leave when she found someone more useful.

And yet there was another part of her that rebelled at the idea. It was like seeing a top racehorse mishandled. Miguel might not think so, but he deserved more out of a relationship than a toss in the hay with Patsy Dimpton. But she had no control over the situation.

"Miguel and I have nothing going," said Sabina.

"Wow, and he's done all that for you just as a friend? Imagine what he'd do . . ."

Sabina didn't want to hear any more. She turned toward the stairs. "Good luck," she called back to Patsy.

"Thanks, I'll let you know how it turns out."

"Spare me the details," Sabina muttered to herself.

"Hey," Patsy called after her. "See you later—at the meeting."

The closer the meeting with San Felipe's manager drew, the less enthusiastic Sabina became about the idea. Even Charlotte's and Patsy's unbridled enthusiasm as they waited in Bob Perile's outer office only increased her doubts. She was sure they would be laughed at and booted out the door.

A secretary ushered them into a plush office. Several chairs were placed opposite a large desk, where the general manager, Bob Perile, was sitting. A bulky man in his fifties, he rose politely to greet them and cordially offered to have his secretary bring them coffee.

As soon as they were all settled with their coffee mugs, he leaned back in his upholstered swivel chair, placed his fingertips together and said pleasantly, "Now, what can I do for you gals?"

"We'd like to have an all-women race here at San Felipe," began Charlotte, who had felt the best strategy was to get to the point as quickly as possible.

Perile leaned forward, bringing his chair down with a soft thud. "All women jockeys out there?"

"That's the idea," said Charlotte.

His mouth smiled, but his eyes didn't. "Let me see if I understand you right. You want a race where all the jockeys will be women."

Sabina wondered why it should take a reasonably intelligent man an inordinate amount of time to grasp a rather simple concept.

"Where would we find that many women jockeys?" he asked.

"There are about two hundred of us across the country," answered Sabina, "and some top riders right here in California. We won't have any trouble filling up a race."

"And think of the publicity value," added Patsy. "It would bring a lot of people out here."

"Now, wait a minute." Perile raised his hand as though to stop traffic. "It's a real cute idea, don't get me wrong. But you girls have to realize that it could leave San Felipe open to a serious charge of reverse discrimination."

"San Felipe's been running all-male races for forty years," said Charlotte, "and you haven't had a lawsuit yet."

Perile scratched his ear. "I don't think you can, uh, look at this like a kind of affirmative action program. Let's be realistic. You can't take guys like Miguel Carrasco or Paul McDonald off horses, substitute a lot of female riders with limited experience and no name draw, and have the same kind of money wagered."

Sabina felt a growing anger. "The reason some of the women jockeys don't have the name draw of a Carrasco or a McDonald is that they don't get the chance to ride the horses those guys do."

"Now, Miss Martin." His voice was soothing. "You certainly can't complain about any discrimination out here at San Felipe. Just the other day you rode one of Bardy Mulligan's horses."

"One horse, one race," snapped Charlotte.

"Any guy with Sabina's talent and ability would be in every race."

The general manager pressed his lips together thoughtfully and cleared his throat. "You certainly cannot fault San Felipe Meadows for that. We have put no obstacles in the way of any woman who's wanted to ride here."

He took a long sip of coffee and then frowned thoughtfully. "This is a difficult track for any jockey to get a mount. You're competing against the very best in the world, the crème de la crème, as it were. Miss Martin, you should feel honored to be riding at all at San Felipe. As soon as there are more girl jockeys of your caliber, I'm sure they will have a chance, too."

"There are plenty of women jockeys of my caliber out there," she shot back. "Some a lot better than I am, too."

He held his hand up like a stop sign again. Had he once been a traffic policeman? Sabina wondered.

"But in any case, girls, this isn't a decision I can make on my own. I'd have to consult the stewards, talk to the publicity department, our lawyers, the board of directors. We send a lot of money to the State of California. They might have to be consulted on this too if it would mean a significant loss of revenue. How about if I check with them and get back to you gals later this week?"

"If we're turned down," Patsy piped up, "we're going to take it to the media. They'd have a field day with it."

Sabina wasn't sure if such a heavy-handed

threat was wise at this point. Then again, they had nothing to lose. She had always been aware of the prejudice that existed against women at the track. It wasn't going to be wiped out overnight.

Ten years before jockeys had threatened to boycott races if women were allowed to ride. She was frankly sick of being reminded how honored she should feel to be at San Felipe. She was good, but there were dozens of women just as good, if not better, who should be competing there. Maybe Charlotte and Patsy were right: what they needed was to stir up some publicity.

She had never done any campaigning for women's issues, although she had been asked to from time to time. Her sympathies were there, but to get involved in politics would have taken too much precious time away from racing. But this issue struck at the heart of her existence, not to mention her dwindling pocketbook.

Bob Perile stood up to signify the end of the meeting. "Well, all I can promise is that I'll take it up with the proper authorities and get back to you." He flashed them each an individual, reassuring smile that didn't fool any of them.

Sabina looked for Miguel's gull-wing Mercedes in the parking lot, but he had evidently left the track. She felt the harsh pang of regret deep in her chest. It was important to talk to him, to set him straight about last night.

She still did not want to speak to him over the phone, and there was no time to stop by his house. This was the day Charlotte had scheduled her to teach the jockey class.

Teaching the class had not been on the top of her list of pleasant pastimes, but the meeting with Bob Perile had given her some inspiration.

She met Patsy and some of the girls at a rental stable in Griffith Park. The magnificent park stretched over hundreds of acres of a wild, untamed portion of the Santa Monica mountains had been a gift to the city of Los Angeles from the colorful, legendary Colonel Griffith at the turn of the century. Despite a freeway that was slashed across its base and a hideous gash in the once scenic Toyon Canyon for a hundred-acre garbage dump, the park remained, overall, a haven for hikers and horsemen, one of the most beautiful stretches of hills and canyons in Southern California.

Sabina had been raised in nearby Burbank and knew almost every inch of the forty miles of riding trails. For the lesson, however, she chose a flat area not far off the Ventura Freeway. The tired old rental horses would be a far cry from the San Felipe mounts, but they were good enough for a lesson in the basics of thoroughbred racing. And since it was a weekday, when business was slow, the stable owner had said he wouldn't mind her using the horses for a jockey class as long as she went easy on them.

Patsy had managed to round up racing saddles and bridles, crops and helmets. Sabina was certain that if Patsy had been asked to round up two battleships and a space shuttle, she could have done that, too, with time to spare. Her kind of determination knew no bounds. And from a quick glance around the class, Sabina had the feeling Patsy wasn't the only one with determination.

Four of the girls were hot walkers, five were grooms. Only Patsy had an excercise license, however dubiously attained. Sabina showed them how to get mounted and "tied on," the process of tying a knot in the reins, tightening the girth and adjusting the stirrups.

She had them leave their stirrups longer than they would be on a normal racing saddle. Race riding was so radically different from the riding most of these girls had done before, they would have to build their muscles up gradually before trying to perch on top of the saddle like a jockey.

Sabina taught them how to "throw a cross," or take a shorter hold of the reins, and how to switch a whip from one hand to the other.

They all had some ability, but it soon became evident that Patsy was the star pupil. Even in the few days she had been exercising Frank's horses, she had improved. She quickly learned and memorized the instructions Sabina gave her. It was rare that she made the same mistake twice. Miguel had joked about the younger girl competing with Sabina, but now Sabina realized it wasn't so farfetched, now that she'd seen what Patsy could do.

When she got back to her apartment that night, she checked for messages. Miguel still hadn't called. She didn't want to postpone it any longer. She had to talk to him.

To bolster her nerve she poured herself a half glass of wine. Any more would be too many calories. Slowly she dialed his number. The maid answered again.

"No, Mr. Carrasco is not here. May I take a message for him?"

"Uh, no. I'll call back. Do you know when he'll be in?"

"I'm sorry. I don't know when to expect him."

Sabina quickly debated leaving a message. She hated to keep calling. "Well, tell him Sabina called," she said.

As it got later and later she began to wonder if she'd done the right thing. If he had received her message, he had decided not to call her. And if he hadn't, he was still out. She wondered who he was with. The thought of him with another woman was almost more excruciating than the possibility that he was deliberately not calling her.

But she had no claim on him. She had made that clear to Patsy.

Patsy. Oh, no, he couldn't!

But why not? Hadn't he bought the other girl a cup of coffee that morning? And with Patsy's determination to get what she wanted. . . .

Stop that, Sabina!

She pulled the pillow over her head and forced her eyes shut, hoping to block out the vision of Miguel and Patsy in that huge bed in front of the fireplace.

Torturing herself wasn't going to do any good. She had never mulled for long over a race she'd lost. You had to keep thinking ahead. She couldn't afford to expend this much thought on a man. She had horses to race the next day, some of the best horses of her life. That was where all her attention should be focused.

If Miguel wanted to hear her explanation of why she had been with Frank Lathrop, he'd call, if not, he wasn't worth it. She would just have to put him out of her mind.

He didn't call that night, but try as she might to erase him from her mind, the next morning she found herself stealing glances over at the stands while galloping horses around the track. It was a dangerous practice. One of her horses, sensing that her attention wasn't fully on him, bolted and nearly threw her.

"A good lesson for me," she mumbled to herself when she had set the horse straight.

When she arrived at clockers' corner for her break, she felt her spirits pick up. Miguel was sitting at a table. Here was her chance to talk to him face to face. Then she saw who was with him.

Patsy Dimpton waved cheerfully. "Come on over and join us for coffee," she called.

Sabina felt the claws of the green-eyed monster grab her by the throat. How was it that Patsy was now inviting her to coffee with Miguel? Had Patsy been with him last night? The thought was almost too horrible to contemplate. Sabina looked for signs that the two of them might be chummier than usual.

Patsy was her usual bubbly self. "I was just telling Miguel about our meeting with the manager of San Felipe. We're supposed to find out today from Bob Perile what the decision is."

Sabina made a quick mental calculation. If Patsy was just telling Miguel about the meeting, it was doubtful she had been with him the night before. Then again, it could be that they hadn't had time to discuss the problems of women jockeys.

"I don't have much hope that San Felipe will go along with us," Sabina commented.

Miguel's expression had not softened. There was a chilling blackness in his eyes. Patsy didn't seem to sense any trouble, and bubbled on. "I was talking to some of the girls, and I think if San Felipe turns us down, we ought to stage a huge strike of all the women at the track. I mean, with all of us here, we could shut the place down! What a news story. It would hit papers all over the world. We'd have TV cameras out here and . . ."

"Hold it, Patsy," said Sabina. "That all sounds very show biz, but it's doubtful a strike would shut San Felipe down. And furthermore, would it do us any good?"

"What do you think, Miguel?" Patsy flashed a dimple and rested a hand on his arm.

He continued to look at Sabina. "That is something the women will have to decide for themselves."

"Well, it would be kind of nice to know what the male jockeys would think of it," pressed Patsy.

"I can't speak for them," said Miguel.

"You can speak for yourself," said Sabina, suddenly annoyed at his reticence.

"I am a jockey by profession, not a public relations expert. I don't know how that kind of publicity would affect you. But you would be wise to find out."

He was still being evasive. Sabina wondered what he really did think of the plan. If San Felipe were to approve an all-woman race, would the men sue the track for reverse discrimination? And if the women did decide to do something as radical as carry off a strike against the track, where would the jockeys stand on the issue? Certainly if the track closed down, they were not likely to look on it favorably. It would cut into their earnings.

Miguel's eyes were still on Sabina. "I got your message too late to return your call last night. Was it important?"

Important? It had been tearing her apart for two days. But she couldn't talk about it in front of Patsy. "Uh, I just wanted to talk to you about something. It can wait."

Patsy suddenly sensed the tension between them. She looked from Miguel to Sabina. "Would you guys like me to leave?"

Miguel put a hand on her arm this time. "No, Patsy, of course not." Sabina's insides churned.

She looked at her watch. "I've got some more horses to gallop," she said, and stood up. "See you."

"Are you racing this afternoon?" he asked.

"Yes. I've got horses in the second and ninth races."

"Pick up the tapes and bring them over when you're through," he said. "We'll take a look and see how you did."

"How nice that you're helping Sabina with her riding!" said Patsy, and then added with a flirtatious sidelong glance at him, "that way Sabina can pass on your tips to us in class."

"How did you do in Sabina's class the other day?" he asked.

"Sabina could tell you better than I could."

"She did extremely well," said Sabina sincerely.

"Oh, you're being too kind," Patsy said coyly. "I thought I was just awful. There's so much to think about: heels down, knees in, hands low, switching the whip, throwing a cross. It's like trying to rub your stomach and pat your head. Of course, I've ridden horses for years, but not like this."

"You get used to it," said Miguel.

"I hope so." She sighed prettily. "Listen, are you going to be doing anything next Monday afternoon?" she asked.

"I doubt it," he answered. "Why?"

"That's when our next class is. I thought maybe you might be able to stop by and give us some pointers, too."

Sabina jumped in to protect him. "I'm sure the last thing Miguel would want to—"

"No, I'd be pleased to come to your class."

Sabina felt the jealousy sinking its fangs in deeper. She wanted him all to herself. His advice to her had been something special and unique, a sharing between friends, and now he was going to hand it willy-nilly to a group of strangers.

Then she felt terrible for begrudging the girls his generosity. Like his honesty, it was a maddeningly admirable trait.

"It would mean so much to us," said Patsy, treating him to a lethal dose of dimples. "You can't imagine!"

The dimples were the final blow. Sabina excused herself and left them sitting there.

No doubt Patsy would take advantage of the situation. At least Sabina could find some consolation in surmising that Patsy had not spent the night with Miguel. He hadn't heard about the meeting with Perile, or about Patsy's lesson. It was unlikely Patsy would have let both these gems slip by, no matter how busy they'd been.

And no matter how much he distrusted or despised her, he was still willing to help her with her riding. She would at least have a chance to explain what she had been doing with Frank.

At noon they were back in the manager's office. Bob Perile was as cordial as ever and once again had his secretary provide them all with coffee.

He began with a patronizing smile. "Everyone thought the idea of an all-women race was just terrific, publicity-wise, but I'm afraid our legal department put the kabosh on it. The lawyers say that it could leave San Felipe open to a charge of reverse discrimination from the other jockeys."

"Have you spoken to the other jockeys?" asked Charlotte.

"Well, no. But you understand. We can't take that chance."

"And you understand that we're taking it to the media?" said Charlotte. "We might even organize a general strike to protest your refusal to grant us the race."

Bob Perile pulled nervously on the knot of his tie. "I can't stop you girls from doing that, but I hope you'll reconsider."

"And we hope you'll reconsider your decision," Charlotte shot back.

Back outside they conferred. "I think we've got him scared," said Patsy.

"Don't be so sure," Charlotte said. "That guy manages millions of dollars a year in revenues. He's no dummy and not so easily intimidated."

As they walked down the stairs back to the stable area Sabina said, "Look, I don't think we should make a circus out of this."

"Are you chickening out?" Charlotte pointed an accusing finger at her. "Does this mean that you won't honor our picket line?"

"All of a sudden we've decided to strike? Whose decision is this?" asked Sabina. "At the meeting we simply decided to take the idea to the track management and see what they said. The other women deserve a vote in this. If we're talking some kind of walkout, jobs are at stake. It's not like holding a damn fashion show, Charlotte. Did you ever stop to consider that the media could look at this as a big joke? A lot of us have been in this a long time, doing our damnedest to build up some credibility in this sport. The media could brand us a bunch of silly publicity seekers and set our cause back ten years."

Charlotte's eyes narrowed. "Sure, you're cautious right now because you're finally getting booked on some good horses, Sabina. But think of the other women, who have never been able to get a horse here. They didn't have any star jockey helping them out."

Patsy jumped into the fray. "You're a fine one to talk about women not getting horses here. What a hypocrite! You're an assistant trainer. You assign jockeys to horses every day. Sabina may be riding a few good horses now, but they sure as hell aren't out of your stable!"

Charlotte's mouth fell open, then clamped shut.

"All right," she said after a moment. "I'll put my money where my mouth is. My boss will scream holy hell, but I've got a horse in the third race tomorrow, Sabina. She's a three-year-old maiden filly, and green as grass. Her regular jockey's out with the flu, and I need a replacement. You want her, you got her."

"I'll take her," said Sabina, with a wink to Patsy. It was strange thinking of Patsy Dimpton as an ally when she had been regarding her as a rival all morning.

Little Patsy wasn't through upbraiding the imperious Charlotte. Sabina had to admit the girl certainly had the guts to be a jockey. "And furthermore, if Sabina doesn't want to go along with this, it's her own damn business. I agree with her. The three of us don't have any right to speak for the rest of the women. A lot of them, myself included, are barely making it by on exercise fees. A week out of work could mean the difference between eating and not eating. We have to have another meeting and take a vote."

Charlotte reluctantly agreed and returned to her barn. Patsy and Sabina walked back to the parking lot.

"I think you missed your calling," Sabina told her.

"You don't think I have the talent to be a jockey?" asked Patsy worriedly.

"You've got the talent, and more guts than

most jockeys I've known, but if you ever decide that racing isn't for you, you'd make one hell of an agent."

Patsy laughed. "You don't think I came on too strong back there in the office, do you?"

"No, you were fine. And I loved the way you bullied Charlotte into giving me a horse."

"She deserved to be bullied," said Patsy. "Oh, by the way, after you left Miguel invited me out to breakfast tomorrow after workouts."

All Sabina's newfound admiration for Patsy vanished at those words, but she tried to pretend they didn't bother her.

"He's got to be one of the sexiest men I've ever met," continued Patsy. "The look he gets in those dark eyes. It makes you feel naked. Don't you find him sexy?"

"I can't imagine anyone who wouldn't," Sabina answered evasively.

"How come you didn't . . . oh, I guess it's none of my business. Hey, see you later."

Chapter 7

SABINA PLACED THIRD IN A FIELD OF TWELVE IN HER
first race of the afternoon and fourth out of a field
of ten in the second. Both trainers were pleased
with the way she had ridden, saying she had done
the best that was possible with the horses she'd
had, but she wasn't happy. She had wanted a win.

After collecting the tapes of the races, she went
home to shower and change. What she would
encounter at Miguel's house was anyone's guess.
It had been surprising that after glaring at her so
coldly he had asked her to come over to view the
tapes.

She slipped into a pale-yellow blouse with a soft
ruffle around its plunging neckline. She washed
and set her chestnut hair, then brushed it until it
hung in becoming silky waves around her shoulders.

Was she dressing to seduce him? It struck her that, subconsciously, she was. She was a born competitor, and Patsy Dimpton had brought out her will to win. But was she ready to cross the finish line? That, she wasn't sure. First she would set him straight about Frank Lathrop, and afterwards . . . well, it was like a race. Sometimes you just had to wait and see how the field shaped up.

Her stomach was growling. Miguel hadn't mentioned anything about having dinner with him, and she wondered whether or not to eat before she went to his house. She gazed longingly at a can of tuna fish, nearly opened it, then decided on a few slices of mozzarella cheese instead. It would be enough protein to sustain her through the viewing of a few tapes, but wouldn't kill her appetite if dinner was served.

The butler greeted her at the door and showed her into Miguel's study. He was at his desk and looked up as she came into the room. The dark eyes had still not lost their coldness.

"You have the tapes with you?" he asked.

She put them on the desk. "Miguel, can we talk first?"

"Certainly." He came out from behind the desk and motioned for her to join him on the couch.

Before she could begin speaking, the maid appeared with a tray of guacamole dip and tortilla chips. Miguel offered her a drink, but she turned it down. He poured himself a straight Scotch and sipped at it slowly.

"What would you like to say, *amigita?*"

"About the night at La Chambre Bleu," she began hesitantly.

"Have some guacamole," he suggested.

"Too fattening," she said. "About La Chambre Bleu," she began again. "I know what you must have been thinking, seeing me there like that with Frank."

He dipped a tortilla chip into the guacamole and slipped a generous portion into his mouth. "It's very good. A small amount won't hurt you. Here." He dipped the chip and handed it to her.

"Well, all right. Don't you worry about getting fat?"

"All the time. Now, what did you think I thought about you and Frank Lathrop?"

"You probably thought I was lying to you about having dinner with my parents, too. You see, my Dad works for the studios, and they needed him on location in San Francisco. It was one of those last-minute things. So they cancelled out, and then Frank called to apologize and said his daughter was in town and . . ."

"You told me you and he didn't even date. That looked very much like a date," Miguel pointed out.

"Frank and I don't date. He's never even taken me to dinner before. Doesn't it seem a little odd that he'd invite his daughter along if he and I were having some kind of torrid affair?"

"A man who was very serious about a woman would want her to meet his daughter," said Miguel.

She was beginning to feel frustrated. "Frank

isn't serious about me. Oh damn it, Miguel, I don't know why you think I'm concocting all this, and what's worse, I don't know why I even care!"

The butler appeared in the doorway. "Excuse me, Mr. Carrasco, but is Miss Martin staying for dinner?"

"Are you?" Miguel turned to her.

"Are you sure you want a concoctor of tall tales at your table?"

"It might be amusing, although for dinner you could try coming up with something a little more exotic. I've always been partial to jungle settings."

"Buxom women draped in leopardskin loincloths riding crocodiles up the Ubangi River?" she suggested dryly.

"Splendid!" He turned to the butler, who had been waiting patiently, trying to suppress a smile. "There will be two of us, John. And see if you can't find my record of Nigerian war drums. We will need some appropriate dinner music as background."

"Yes, sir."

"You really have a record of Nigerian war drums?" she asked incredulously as John left the room.

"You'd prefer Tanzanian war drums?"

"Don't be silly. Next to Mozart, there is nothing I adore like Nigerian war drums. They'll be superb for the digestion."

He laughed and took her hand. "I don't know why I should believe that story about Frank, but I do."

"Then you're not angry at me anymore?"

"It was the Spanish blood," he said. "I was

jealous. I wanted to take Frank apart limb by limb."

Sabina shuddered. "He's not a bad guy, really. He just had his priorities a little confused. I think he's straightened away now."

"And what about you?" He rubbed his thumb over the back of her hand. "Are your priorities straightened away too?"

The butler returned to announce that the jungle drums were on the stereo and dinner was on the table.

Candles were lit, the chandelier turned down. Crisp spinach salads were brought in on chilled salad plates.

"Just out of idle curiosity," she said as she lifted the monogrammed fork, "do you ever open a can of tuna fish in the kitchen?"

"Never," he said, raising a wine goblet to her in a toast. "Although there was a time as a child that I was so hungry I would have held a knife to someone's throat for a can of tuna fish. It is one of life's ironies that now, when I can afford all the food I want, I often go hungry just to keep my weight down."

Flutes suddenly joined the jungle drums. "Where in the world did you get these recordings?" she asked.

"Africa. I've been several times. Fascinating place. Now, what are the stories you had for me?"

The stories, jokes and tall tales continued through dinner until she was laughing so hard, tears were rolling down her face. They were still chuckling as they went back to his den to look at the tapes of her races.

"Where did you learn so many jokes?" he asked her.

She thought about Al, and the memory of those nights suddenly made her sad. "Oh, from a guy I used to know."

"A jockey?"

"Yeah. Let's look at those tapes. In that first race I thought I had enough horse to get rolling around the first turn."

He loaded the cassette, but his attention was not on the race. He was watching her. "Tell me about him, Sabina."

"He broke sharply from the gate and . . ."

"Not the horse, the jockey. The one who told jokes."

"I'd rather talk about the race."

She bit her lip and tried to concentrate on the TV screen, but she wasn't seeing that race. She was remembering the other one.

Miguel placed his thumb under her chin and lifted her face to him. "I want to know about him."

"Why?"

"I saw the way you looked a moment ago when you mentioned him, the way you look now. I was wrong about Frank Lathrop, but not about your still being in love with some man. Am I right?"

She nodded.

"What is his name?"

"Al. Look, Miguel, you don't really want to hear about this." She tried to sound flip, but it was impossible to pretend with Miguel.

"You are wrong. I want to know all about him." Again he demonstrated the same persistence that made horses do the impossible for him.

"We were together about eight years, until right before I came out to San Felipe."

"What happened? Why did you leave?"

The race playing on the screen and Miguel's prodding was bringing it all back to her, the drizzly, godforsaken fairgrounds, the muddy track, the half-empty grandstands, the seedy track regulars marking up their Racing Forms.

Her skin suddenly felt icy. Miguel was rubbing her arms to warm her. His voice was soothing. "You loved him, Sabina. Why did you leave him?"

"I didn't leave him." Her voice faltered. She brushed away a tear. "There was an accident."

Miguel took her trembling hands in his. "The accident," he prodded her gently.

Knowing Miguel would eventually pull it out of her, she continued haltingly. "I was standing at the rail when it happened. His horse broke a leg and went down. Al was flung against the rail not far from me. I could . . ." Her voice broke off.

"Tell me, *amigita*." He cradled her head against his chest.

"I could . . . see his face."

"What happened to him?"

"He broke an arm, a leg and his neck, but at the hospital, they gave the cause of death as a heart attack."

She could no longer keep back the tears. Miguel held her and let her cry. "The other day, Miguel, when you were flung against the rail . . . I froze up. It was so much like the other time. And sometimes when I'm at the starting gate . . ."

"It's only natural. We all feel that way sometimes. If you'd had less courage, you would have quit racing."

"I can't imagine not racing. But I had to get out of the midwest. I had to get away from the memories there."

"And racing keeps the grief at bay," he added. "I know all about that. As long as you keep racing the pain can't touch you." There was a heavy sadness in his dark eyes. He was feeling her grief and his own.

"Is that why you want so badly to get back out there?" she asked softly.

"Stay with me, tonight, Sabina."

"I don't know. . . ."

"You see an accident on the track, and you have the courage to keep racing. You lose someone you love, but you must keep loving."

He cupped her face in his strong hands and brushed the tears away from the corners of her eyes with his thumbs, then kissed her.

She clung to him, a desperate need for him filling her.

Taking her hand, he led her up the winding staircase to his room.

Chapter 8

THERE WAS ONLY FIRELIGHT IN THE ROOM. THE golden shadows danced on the walls and spilled onto the satin sheets.

As she lay back against the profusion of pillows he slowly unbuttoned her pale-yellow silk blouse, as though unveiling a wondrous treasure. Under his sultry gaze the tips of her breasts grew taut. Her breathing became ragged as his mouth claimed them, tasting, circling, blowing lightly on them.

Darts of passion shot through her. She felt her body arching as her fingers wound through his thick black hair.

"Mi amor," he whispered as his lips followed the graceful curve of her neck.

"Miguel. . . ."

The way she moaned his name seemed to

enflame him as his mouth came down on hers. Pulling her to him, he slid the blouse off her shoulders, down over her arms and flung it aside.

Wanting to feel his skin against hers, she fumbled with the buttons of his shirt, but her fingers were shaking.

"Let me," he said, and gently kissed the tips of her trembling fingers one by one.

His shirt off, she ran her hand down the strongly muscled chest, the coarse chest hair making the palms of her hands tingle.

His fingers were at the zipper of her pants, slipping inside. He did not remove the garment immediately, but let the sensation of material rubbing against her skin along with his caresses arouse her.

Then, as he slid the pants over her hips, he bent over her. His lips were at her navel, and lowered to her belly as the pants slowly progressed over her thighs and legs and ankles.

Her confining clothes were being stripped away like inhibitions. There was nothing to hold them apart anymore. She would give whatever he asked and hold nothing back.

His mouth was on the satiny smooth inside of her thigh. She could feel the light grazing of teeth as he nibbled, gently provoking spiraling sensations that flooded the lower half of her body.

His strong, sure hands swept down her legs, and they parted for him.

Sabina's head was flung back against the pillows and she moaned at the beauty of his love. Her body was now completely his, captivated and trembling, twisting according to his wishes.

She was vaguely aware of his mouth, his fingers, but what they were doing exactly, she didn't know. It was her own body that she was experiencing, as never before, and the spectrum of sensations was limitless.

Until then she had thought the greatest excitement was to be had from riding at full speed down the track. But this was even more breathtaking, and she had no control. It was like losing a bridle at the starting gate. All she could do was hang on for her life until it was over.

Just when she thought she had reached the limit of her endurance, he whirled her around so that her knees slipped down on either side of him. He was guiding her hips, lowering her over himself. She felt a tremor unlike anything she had felt before, and she moved to capture it again and again. In his dark eyes, she could see the reflection of her own love.

"Mi alma," he whispered, bringing her face down to his.

Wrapping her legs around his strong back, he turned her around again and plunged deeper, the rhythm increasing like jungle drums.

Her fingers dug into the thick muscles of his strong shoulders, her legs tightened around his back. They were spinning madly like fiery comets across a black satin sky strewn with glittering diamonds.

Later, as she lay trembling in his arms, he twisted damp tendrils of her long hair through his fingers and smiled down on her. "How do you feel?" he asked her.

"Loved," she answered him.

"You are. Do you know I have wanted you since I saw you ride your first race at San Felipe?"

"I came in last!"

"You were magnificent. It was amazing that nag of Frank's even made it around the track. But you rode beautifully."

"How come you never asked me out?"

"Would you have accepted?"

"Probably not. I was still recovering from Al. I wasn't dating anyone."

"Tell me about him."

She was hesitant at first, but found she could talk about him at last without tears. She conjured up a picture of him in her head, the boyish shock of blond hair, the lopsided grin. "We met when I first started racing. Both of us were away from home for the first time. It seemed like a grand adventure. And it was. I guess we kind of grew up together."

"Were you married?"

She smiled. "We were always about to do that. Then he'd get some good mounts at one racetrack and I'd get them at another. When you're traveling so much, sometimes it's hard to get together. We weren't in any hurry to have kids, so it wasn't that important."

She rested her head on his chest and looked at the fire. "Have you ever been close to marrying someone?"

"Natasha," he said quietly. "And if you hadn't showed up at San Felipe, I might have. I knew I couldn't love her and feel the way I did about you. I've never felt this way about any woman before. You walk into a room and I can't keep my eyes off you. Hardly a moment goes by when I'm not thinking about you."

She turned to look up at him. "Even on the track?"

He grinned. "All right. There are a few moments I put you out of my mind. But when I went down the other day on Composure, the first thing I worried about was whether you were okay. I don't know what I would have done if that bumping had caused you an injury."

She put her head back on his chest and stroked his strong forearm. She knew how that was. The fear for someone you loved was worse than the fear for your own skin. It was worse because you had no control over it.

Miguel shifted his weight so that their faces nearly touched. As he kissed her she could feel his readiness to make love again. His hands swept down her sides and over her buttocks. She moaned and buried her lips in the hollow of his neck.

Pulling herself up on her knees, she straddled him and, finding his male hardness, slid down gently, feeling the rainbow invade her.

He stroked her breasts and her belly as she moved on him slowly, wringing as much pleasure out of him as possible. His fingers, finding the center of her desire, rubbed in the same slow, sensuous rhythm.

She threw her head back and reveled in the sensations, thinking it was like riding a thoroughbred across a dawn meadow.

They were both agile athletes. Their legs bent and their muscles stretched as their love took on new forms, changing shapes like lazy, summer clouds. Sabina was not aware that lovemaking could be like this, unhurried and full of discovery. They teased each other with their tongues and teeth.

Her skin shone golden in the firelight. There were fragrances of love to savor and taste, textures to explore—the sandpaper roughness of his jaw, the hard strength of his muscled thighs.

But their need was too strong to prolong the lazy stroking. And as her desire increased, he gave her more, plunging into her depths.

The need intensified, driving them violently to the brink. She clutched at his back as they slammed against each other, begging for completion and yet wanting it never to end.

When it came, she groaned and trembled, feeling him with her, gasping and shuddering against her. They lay together in awe of their own power.

"My God, Sabina," he said, disengaging them finally. "How I love you." He kissed her damp forehead, then sprawled back on the pillows.

"How do you feel, Miguel?"

He grinned at her. "Exhausted. How about you?"

"Exhausted, too. Oh, no." She suddenly remembered what time she had to be at the track in the morning. "What time is it?"

"About two A.M."

"We've been at this a long time," she said with wonder.

He ran a caressing hand down the length of her, and she shuddered from the evocative pleasure it brought back.

"I have to go to work tomorrow morning," she

protested. "And you've gotten me so I don't think I can walk, much less ride."

"No," he said logically. "This is good for your riding muscles. Increases your stamina. But I will let you go to sleep."

He turned her away from him and wrapped himself protectively around her, crossing his arms over her breasts. The warmth of him enveloped and soothed her. Then he kissed her gently on her shoulder. "Sleep well, my love," he said.

And she did.

Morning came too soon. She was disoriented for a moment, looking around at the large room, the man beside her, turning off a digital alarm.

"Miguel . . . I don't think I can make it."

He sat up in bed and shook his head, as though to clear it. "Sure, you can. I'll go run the shower. You'll feel like a new person. Then we'll go downstairs and pour some coffee into you and send you on your way."

"How come you feel so chipper?" she complained, "when I just want to curl back up here in bed and go back to sleep."

"I know that as soon as you leave, I can come back up here and go to sleep."

She threw a pillow at him but followed obediently into the bathroom.

Floor to ceiling white marble, the room was as large as her apartment bedroom. In the center, under a skylight, was a large hexagonal Jacuzzi surrounded by tropical plants.

Sabina gazed at it longingly as he adjusted the shower. "Not this morning," said Miguel, pulling her toward the shower.

"You're cruel and inhuman," she mumbled.

He joined her in the shower and placed her solidly under the water. She gazed around at the shower stall. "You could fit half a dozen people in here," she said.

He laughed, then lathered her up with soap and rinsed her off. "There you are," he said proudly, "like new."

"I feel old," she grumbled as he rubbed her dry with a bath towel.

They went downstairs and into the kitchen, where he fixed her a cup of instant coffee. "I am afraid this is the extent of what I do for myself," he said.

"Then I'm flattered that you're doing it for me."

"It's too early for the maid to be up," he explained. "Otherwise I would have seen that you had breakfast in bed. Another day."

"How about breakfast in the Jacuzzi?"

"Champagne breakfast in the Jacuzzi."

"No jungle drums, though," she said.

He agreed.

It was still dark when he walked her out to her car in his bathrobe. The air was damp; rain was in the offing. "Darling, you're going to get chilled," she said to him.

"Don't worry." He leaned into the car window and kissed her lightly on the lips. "Drive carefully and ride even more carefully when you get out to the track. I could never live with myself if I heard you got sleepy and fell off."

"I wouldn't think of it," she promised him.

"When is your next race?"

"Tomorrow afternoon."

He looked at the ominous dark clouds gathering overhead. "It may rain. I want to show you some tapes of races run on that track in the rain. But while you're out there today, notice that the springiest part of the track is right down the center. San Felipe wasn't always that way. I used to get the most speed along the rail when it was muddy. I don't know why it's changed, but it has. I discovered it by chance a few months ago. It's not something many jockeys are aware of yet. Keep it to yourself."

"Thanks, darling. Are you going out to the track this morning to watch workouts?"

"Yes, as a matter of fact I have a breakfast appointment with someone. So I may see you at break." He kissed her again, this time a little longer. "'Bye, my love."

She put the car in gear and sighed. What a night! In her wildest fantasies she would not have imagined what had happened.

Recalling the details as she waited at a stoplight, she became so absorbed that she missed the light turning green and was rudely brought down to earth by the horn of the car behind her.

Changing quickly into her jeans, she grabbed another half cup of coffee at her apartment and headed back to the track.

Patsy Dimpton pulled into the parking space beside her. Ah, Patsy, she thought, if you only knew.

Patsy! My God! The breakfast appointment. She had almost forgotten that Miguel had invited Patsy to breakfast.

Patsy, however, was not long in reminding her. "I'm really excited," she said. "I'm going to try to

talk him into taking a stand on the women's
jockey race. Can you imagine the kind of clout
we'd have if Miguel Carrasco came out in favor of
it?"

True to form, Patsy was still only interested in
what she could get out of Miguel.

"I don't think we should try to pressure any of
the guys," said Sabina. "If they want to help us
out, they will. But it's not really their issue, it's
ours. Did Charlotte get another meeting scheduled so that we can take a vote?"

"Thursday night. I've been talking it up,
though, and I think everyone is in favor."

Sabina wasn't pleased. Staging a protest was a
major move. And it would come at a time when
she was just beginning to make some progress at
San Felipe.

There was always the chance, if the strike was
effective, that the trainers would be angered and
refuse to hire her at all. Like Perile, they would
consider her an ingrate for protesting when she
was getting good mounts.

Patsy, Charlotte, the exercise and pony girls
really had nothing to lose but some paychecks.
But if she were thrust into the limelight with
national TV coverage—and she certainly would
be, as the only woman jockey at San Felipe—the
word would quickly get back to the tracks where
she used to ride. She could end up not only with
closed doors at San Felipe, but also with the
trainers in the Midwest considering it risky to hire
her.

Focusing attention on the plight of women
jockeys was a worthwhile cause. She couldn't
argue with that. She just wished some other

woman jockey could be the focus. It was a selfish sentiment, she knew, but being able to race was still more important than any cause. She could see herself getting pressured into this and coming out with nothing.

Miguel was not at clockers' corner during the eight o'clock break. Had he gone back to bed, as he had threatened? She was hoping he had. She fervently wished he would sleep soundly through his breakfast date with Patsy.

In fact, he would probably cancel it. He couldn't still be interested in Patsy, not after last night. Or could he?

How well did she really know Miguel Carrasco? Maybe one woman wasn't enough. There were Don Juans who could say "I love you" with equal sincerity to any woman. And in spite of the passion of the previous evening, the sincere-sounding murmurs of love and a vague promise of a champagne Jacuzzi breakfast, there had been no assurances about the future.

As she checked the saddle on her next mount Patsy rushed up to her. "Miguel just called me down at Frank's barn," she confided excitedly. "He said he slept late and wasn't able to get over here, so he wants me to meet him at his house. His *house!* Can you imagine? It's like an open invitation. He says we can have breakfast there. Imagine having breakfast in Miguel's Carrasco's house! The girls are going to be livid with jealousy when I tell them."

Sabina bit her lower lip to keep it from quivering. "I'm sure they will be."

"Well, wish me luck," said Patsy breathlessly and rushed off without waiting for the wish.

It was just as well. Sabina was seething. How dare he have someone else to his house not more than a few hours after she'd been there! There wouldn't even be time to have the maid change the satin sheets.

She was so shaken that she nearly missed seeing a dangerous tear in the bridle. It was one thing to compare making love to Miguel to racing without a bridle, but she had ridden with a broken bridle a few times, and it was terrifying to be racing down the track with no control. While the groom was replacing it she leaned an arm on Xenophon, the big colt she was growing so attached to.

He already knew that she could be counted on for a scratch on the withers, and twisted around so that she could accommodate him. While she scratched he nuzzled her back, making kissing motions with his mouth.

"You horses are wonderful," she said to him as they headed out to the track. "A good scratch on the withers is all it takes to make you happy. What is it with these damn men?"

Xenophon blew out his nose and bobbed his head up and down. In agreement, she supposed.

She could have almost forgiven Miguel's taking Patsy out to breakfast. After all, he had asked her out yesterday, before they had made love. He had the kind of integrity that would require he keep a date once it was made. But inviting Patsy to his house was inexcusable.

Fortunately, riding brought back her sense of equilibrium. Xenophon was still inexperienced, a big oversized kid who was still growing. It took him some time to get his huge body coordinated and moving in rhythm, but once he did, he was like lightning.

He had a coltish sense of curiosity, especially about interesting mares galloping by. It wasn't always easy to keep his mind on running.

But no matter what the problems, he was still the highlight of her morning. He had a wonderful disposition and a mouth so sensitive that only a slight movement of her fingers was necessary to relay a message. And unlike some horses she rode, he tried very hard to please her.

When she finished galloping him, she let him satisfy his curiosity for a few minutes by turning him to face the track, a little reward for performing so well. His ears perked up as he watched the other horses working out.

"One day I'm going to race you," she said to him as she patted his neck. "And I hope that bastard Carrasco is in the race. We'll leave him in the dust at the starting gate, and he'll never catch us. What do you say to that, big horse?"

Xenophon made a grunting sound. She scratched his withers. It would not surprise her to learn that horses did understand more than they let on. People who thought they were dumb animals didn't know them very well.

By the time she had finished exercising her last horse, the rain was coming down in large drops. She rushed out to the parking lot, hoping to avoid the rain and Patsy on her way to breakfast.

The more she thought about that breakfast, the angrier she became. Was this part of the same game he had been playing that night with Natasha? He was under the impression that she and

Patsy were friends. He would have to know that Patsy would tell her what was going on.

Then she wondered if she wasn't just being childishly possessive. That very first night she had seen how much he enjoyed entertaining in his home. Just because a woman was going to his house for breakfast, that didn't necessarily mean he meant to seduce her—no matter what Patsy thought.

With that comforting thought to calm her, all she needed was a hot bath and a cup of chamomile tea, combined with her total exhaustion, to send her to sleep the moment her head hit the pillow.

It took a moment for the sound of the door bell to penetrate her slumber. She had been having a nightmare that she was in Miguel's bedroom in the midst of a wild party. Everyone was dressed in jockey silks with helmets and goggles. She was searching for Miguel, but each time she thought it was he, the jockey would take off his helmet and goggles and it would be a stranger, laughing at her, as though she were the butt of some cruel practical joke.

The door bell was persistent, followed by knocking. Not bothering with a bathrobe, she stumbled out of the bedroom toward the door.

"Who is it?"

"Miguel."

After her dream, she was so relieved to see him, she flung open the door and threw her arms around his neck before he could step inside. He hugged her so tightly she was afraid for a moment he'd crack a rib.

"You've been sleeping, *amigita*." He stepped back to look at her, his gaze sliding over the soft curves of the pale-pink nightgown. "Let's put you back in bed."

He flung an arm around her shoulders and led her back to the bedroom. Before she could remember that she was angry at him, he had lifted the nightgown over her head and was raining kisses on her naked skin. "Even better than I remembered," he murmured. "It seems like an eternity since I've seen you."

Although the anger was slowly returning, her body was responding to him, crowding it out. In seconds he was also naked and beside her on the rumpled bed, his strong hands sweeping over her.

The tip of a breast was in his mouth. She was already shuddering, her legs twisting around his. Cupping her breasts in his hands, drawing the sensitive tips taut with his fingers, his mouth moved down over her belly.

She had to ask him about Patsy. She had to know now before they went any further. She couldn't let him make love to her like this if he had been with Patsy that morning. It wasn't fair. It wasn't . . .

His hands gripped the insides of her thighs, pushing them apart as he kneaded them. She felt the warm gusts of his breath. The lower half of her body was arching toward his mouth.

Somehow she had to stop him, stop the betrayal of her own body. She pushed her thighs against his hands to close them, but he was strong, and the pressure there only increased her passion.

With a gasp she realized it was already too late. The erotic sensations were spiraling from her core, welding her to him. His strong hands swept back and forth along the insides of her thighs, under to her hips, lifting her to him. His mouth and fingers were all working to increase her pleasure, rubbing, probing, caressing.

When he finally entered her, she cried out, clutching desperately at his hard back, her mouth on his shoulder.

"Miguel . . . Miguel," she murmured.

He lifted himself and drove slowly, deep inside her, circling and driving in again and again. With each thrust her whole body trembled.

"Do you like that, my darling?"

"Yes," she whispered, reaching up to touch his face and trace the line of his smile. He bit her fingertip gently. She couldn't help thinking that from that angle, his face was even more handsome.

But again she thought about Patsy. Had he made love to her like this?

As her passion increased, she began to wonder recklessly if it really mattered. If he could love her like this when they were together, why should she care if he had another woman, or twenty other women? Who was she to think she could demand exclusivity of such a magnificent man?

As these thoughts floated through her mind she realized with a painful tug that she was beyond thinking rationally about him. He was capable of making her give up every preconceived idea of what a relationship should be. She was willing to take him no matter what the conditions. It was a dangerous position to be in. Emotionally she was vulnerable. She was in love.

They were no longer satisfied with slow, sensuous thrusts. Their bodies were demanding a race, a wild, frantic race. She held nothing back from him, giving everything, every breath and pulse beat.

They held each other for a long time afterward. And it was only when they had rolled apart that she began thinking about Patsy again. The unconditional love that she had sworn him while in the throes of passion was suddenly not so binding.

"I didn't see you at the track this morning," she began, hoping to prompt a response. She did not want to seem probing.

"I went back to sleep after you left," he said with a smile. "I thought I was in pretty good shape, but you tired me out last night. Are you going to tire me out again tonight?"

So he wasn't even going to admit being with Patsy! The anger returned in even greater force than before. Keeping her face expressionless, she said, "Did you wake up in time for your breakfast appointment?"

"Barely. Since I was running so late, I changed the meeting place to my house."

He was going to let her think he had some kind of business appointment. This was really too much to take.

And yet she did not want to appear jealous. It was such a base, childishly possessive response. She would have to struggle to keep a veneer of indifference.

"Are you hungry?" he asked.

"Mmmm. I guess a little."

"I know a wonderful little Italian restaurant.

Oh, speaking of restaurants, tomorrow night some of us thought we'd drive up the coast for seafood. How does that sound to you?"

"I've got a meeting of the San Felipe Women's Auxiliary tomorrow night. We're getting our training in machine gun assembly." She had to admit, she felt militant.

Miguel laughed. "Yes, I saw your friend Patsy this morning. That was my breakfast appointment. I got an earful about the cause. She can be quite persuasive."

Sabina sat bolt upright in bed. This was the end. He didn't have to throw Patsy in her face! She realized she was no longer thinking rationally. A minute ago she had been suspicious because he hadn't mentioned Patsy. But now that he had, and in so casual a way, all the burning jealousy came suddenly to the surface, making her tremble with rage.

During her relationship with Al she had been sheltered from the traumas most of her friends were experiencing with men. In fact, one of her close friends had sat her down after the funeral and tried to warn her about what to expect when she began dating again.

At the time, dating seemed so remote that she had turned a deaf ear to Missy's advice. She should have listened more closely. This was exactly the kind of situation Missy, a fellow jockey, had described in chilling detail.

"You're going out to California where the situation is even more bleak than in the rest of the world," Missy had cautioned. "The statistics there are five women for every man. Any good-looking guy can have a harem if he wants, and he'll think he's doing you a favor by including you. Sabina, you think you're savvy because you can go into a horse race prepared for a whole bag of dirty tricks, but take you off a horse, and you're a babe in the woods."

Miguel's behavior was proving the truth of Missy's warning. She had no idea how to cope with his treachery. "Patsy was at your house this morning?" Sabina blurted out, forgetting her veneer of indifference.

"Yes, she was." He sat up slowly and put his hands on her shoulders. "She wanted to talk about the women's protest—lobbying, she called it. And I was interested to hear what she had to say. *Mi amor*, you don't think that Patsy and I . . ."

"You invited her to your house!"

"I invite many people to my house. I enjoy having people there. That is the way I live. I would much rather entertain in my own home. For too many years I slept in stables, on the street. Having a home where I can bring friends is a blessing I do not take lightly."

"But Patsy . . ."

He was looking at her as though she were mad.

"You don't think I could make love to her after making love to you? Sabina!"

Could she trust him? He put such store by honesty, but perhaps that, too, was a lie. After all, she was dealing with a man considered to be one of the best jockeys in the world. Who was to say he wasn't also one of the best lovers? Or the best liar?

"You didn't make love to her?"

He gazed down at her angrily. "Sabina, I love you. Doesn't that mean anything to you?"

It occurred to her that he was still not answering her question directly, but suddenly she didn't want to know any more. She wanted to believe he loved her, that he wouldn't lie to her. No doubt if Missy were there, she would give her a sound lecture on being so gullible.

Instead, Sabina let him pull her back down to the bed. She wrapped her arms around him and gave herself to his kisses.

They made love again, then showered together and went to dinner at Miguel's Italian restaurant.

It was raining hard when they returned to his house. "I'll get those tapes out," he said. "I want you to see how the horses move on that track when it's wet. You're riding Marshall George. He's never run well on the mud. There's a good chance Bardy may scratch him, but you might as well be prepared."

By morning there was only a light drizzle, and the weather forecasts were calling for clearing in the afternoon.

As Sabina exercised horses, she tried out Miguel's theory about the center of the track. It was hard to tell, because she wasn't racing against other horses. The mud would make a slow track in any case, but his advice might pay off. It would be worth a try.

The clouds were beginning to clear earlier than predicted, and strong sunlight was already drying out the track when she met with Bardy. He had decided to leave the horse in the race.

As she was leaving Bardy's stable she saw Patsy Dimpton coming toward her. Miguel had done a good job of convincing her that nothing had gone on between them the previous morning, but Sabina was less certain of his fidelity than she would have liked.

"Hi, Patsy. What's new?"

Patsy's blue eyes widened. "That house!"

"Miguel's?" Sabina asked casually. As if she didn't know.

"It's an estate. I couldn't believe it. He even has servants. A butler and a maid. A butler! I thought they only existed in movies. Imagine somebody having a butler! You could float the whole sixth fleet in that pool and still have room for an oil tanker or two. And the bathhouse. That bathhouse is bigger than any house I've ever lived in."

"Did you . . . uh . . . make any progress?" Sabina hated herself for asking, but she had to.

Patsy's eyes lit up. "That Miguel Carrasco is probably the sexiest hunk of man that ever sat a horse. Talk about sensuous. He's even got a fireplace in the bedroom."

Sabina swallowed hard. "How lovely."

"That's not all. There's a Jacuzzi in his bathroom. Well, you can't really call it a bathroom. Not like any bathroom I've ever seen. There's a skylight above and hanging plants—real ferns, not plastic ones—all around it. Listen, I'd love to tell you all the details, but I'm working a horse for Frank in a few minutes, and you know how he gets if you're late. I don't want him yelling at me. You going to the meeting tonight?"

Sabina nodded.

"Good. I'll tell you all about what happened then. Whew, is that Miguel something! I don't know why you didn't ever get anything going with him. Any woman who had that chance would have to be crazy not to take it."

All the way back to her apartment Sabina fought the tears, trying to tell herself that Miguel wasn't lying.

Patsy hadn't actually said she'd been to bed with him, but what the hell was she doing in his bedroom and Jacuzzi? She'd only been invited for breakfast. The words, "Whew, is that Miguel something!" kept echoing in Sabina's ears.

The phone was ringing when she walked in the door. What if it was Miguel? She let the answering machine pick it up, then listened in.

It was Miguel. He was wishing her luck in the race, telling her he'd be there to watch. "Don't forget, *amigita*, the center of the track is the quickest way home."

She couldn't eat anything for lunch, not that she needed it, she thought, after that Italian dinner. She could have done without the side plate of ravioli.

As she headed back to the track she forced Miguel out of her mind. She'd deal with him later. For the moment the upcoming race had to have her full attention.

It was to be a mile and an eighth, and with the condition of the track, horses slogging through the mud were bound to tire early.

The four-year-old colt named Marshall George had shown excellent promise as a two-year-old, but his career since then had been sporadic. His last workout showed him in moderately good condition. He might do well if the mud didn't get him down.

Gray storm clouds were shifting ominously overhead as they paraded to post. The brief sunshine earlier had been illusory. A few drops of rain splashed onto the track. By the time they were at the starting gate, it was raining steadily.

"Just what this track needs," grumbled the jockey in the next chute, "more mud."

Because of the mud, the jockeys were all wearing four sets of goggles instead of the normal two for a dry track.

Soon after the start, she took Marshall George back to ninth place in the field of ten, letting him relax and keeping him wide all the way down the backstretch. Around the turn, just as Miguel had predicted, the early leaders who had been keeping on the rail began to tire and fall back. Marshall George was anxious to move, but she held him in.

Two more horses took the lead, keeping on the inside; they, too, soon faltered. Then in the last sixteenth, she woke up Marshall George with a tap of the whip that sent him flying past the others down the center of the track. Everything Miguel had told her was dead right. The center was the shortest way home.

She was sailing, flying with the wind on wings of a euphoria so thrilling she wondered how she could have ever thought sex, even with Miguel, could compare. There was nothing in the world more exciting than crossing the finish line a full two lengths ahead of the nearest horse.

It was her first win at San Felipe.

Mud-splattered from head to toe, the pouring rain plastering her racing silks to her body, she grinned for her picture in the winners' circle.

"I didn't know what was wrong out there at first," admitted Bardy, as they walked back through the tunnel. "It wasn't like Marshall George to lag so far behind, even in the mud, but when I saw you moving up there in the final stretch, I figured you knew what you were doing. I'd never have figured that horse for a mudder."

As they walked out of the tunnel she saw Miguel coming toward them. And try as she might to keep cool, her heart was pounding. She only wished she weren't so covered with mud.

He hugged her, mud and all, dirtying his own slacks and raincoat. "Magnificent, Sabina!" He turned to Bardy with pride. "What did you think of our girl, eh?"

"Not bad," said Bardy with a twinkle in his eyes.

"Go get changed," Miguel said to Sabina outside the jockey room, "and we'll go upstairs to the Turf Club for a drink to celebrate."

He looked so handsome, mud and all, that it was painful to resist his invitation.

"I don't really have clothes for The Turf Club," she said evasively. It was a standing joke at San Felipe that the Turf Club dress code was stricter than that of Buckingham Palace.

"Then we'll go to the clubhouse," he said quickly.

"No, thanks. I have some things to take care of at home," she said reluctantly. "I'll catch you later."

He gave her a hard, appraising look. "What is it, Sabina?"

"Nothing." She turned away from him.

"No, there is something bothering you." He took her hand and whirled her around. "What is the matter?"

"I just don't have time for a drink. That's all."

Miguel didn't look as though he believed her. "Call me when you get home from your meeting tonight. I want you to tell me what is bothering you."

Chapter 9

THE WOMEN AT THE MEETING THAT NIGHT WERE excited about her win. It struck her that now, after her first victory at San Felipe, she had even more to lose by joining the protest. And she was even less convinced of its effectiveness. What she had done that afternoon, winning on a slow track with a horse that wasn't supposed to be a good mudder, would do more to elevate women's reputations as jockeys at San Felipe than any staged publicity stunt.

But as she sat back and listened to Charlotte describe the meeting with Bob Perile, she realized that the mood in the room was shifting dramatically in favor of a protest.

Charlotte wasn't relating anything that hadn't happened in the meeting, but her saracasm was painting Bob Perile as a chauvinist ogre. Perile would not be Sabina's choice of a man likely to go out campaigning for the Equal Rights Amendment, but he was nothing more than a functionary echoing some legitimate legal concerns of his employers. And in his annoyingly patronizing way, he had been a gentleman.

But each time Charlotte quoted Perile as using the word "girls," the women in the room became more indignant. Several of them booed and hissed.

Patsy went to the front of the room and while confirming everything that Charlotte said, added a few asides that made Perile seem positively villainous. "The attitude of these track officials is outrageous," she said angrily. "We can't let them get away with this!"

Bonnie, who was sitting in the back row next to Sabina, raised her hand. "Has anybody talked to the jockeys? How do we know they wouldn't sue the track?"

A mysterious smile crossed Patsy's face. Her eyes twinkled as she and Charlotte exchanged glances. "Should I tell them now or wait until after we've taken a vote?" Patsy asked Charlotte.

"Oh, to heck with it." A cat-that-ate-the-canary smile lit up Charlotte's face. "Tell them now."

"Well, we were going to wait, because we didn't want this to influence you," said Patsy, "but I had a long, highly productive talk with Miguel Carrasco and convinced him to lend us his full support."

"Just what we need," said Bonnie wryly. "A jockey supporter."

Everyone laughed.

Bonnie turned to Sabina and whispered, "I wonder what persuasive technique little Patsy used to get that concession out of Carrasco."

Patsy was continuing brightly. "With Miguel Carrasco behind us, we are sure to get national attention. And I'm sure he'll get all the other jockeys on our side. He's the most respected jockey on the track. We won't have any trouble with lawsuits."

"What do you think, Sabina?" asked Charlotte. "Are you with us?"

Sabina was too stunned with Patsy's latest revelations to utter a word. Patsy must have been persuasive indeed. Miguel's sudden turnaround certainly hadn't been caused by anything Sabina had said. As far as she could remember, they hadn't even discussed the women's race.

"Well, what do you say, Sabina?" Patsy pressed.

She felt like protesting, all right, but not about the plight of women jockeys. At the moment she was more concerned about the injustices meted out by all the good-looking Don Juans and Don Miguels of the world. But looking at it rationally, if Miguel and the other jockeys were behind the race, San Felipe would have to reconsider. It was worth a try.

"I'm with you." Yet even as she said the words, she wondered if she'd regret them.

"Super! Let's take a vote. How many in favor?"

The ayes were unanimous. Suddenly Sabina had an ominous vision of Heidi Sioux, Gusty

Guy, Marshall George and Xenophon all sprouting wings and flying away from her forever. She felt a little sick inside. What had she committed herself to?

"Now, let's decide when we're gonna pull this thing off," said Patsy excitedly, as though she were planning to stage a bank robbery.

Most were in favor of walking out on a Sunday, the busiest racing day, when the loss of the women would produce the most havoc for the track.

But Charlotte disagreed. "I've looked into the PR ramifications of this. There are seven TV stations in Los Angeles, but only three of them have weekend film crews. If we want the most coverage, we've got to stage this on a weekday."

By the time she finished rattling off the rest of her research data, the women were convinced the best day would be the following Wednesday. There would be time enough to make all the necessary phone calls, get out the press releases, have the T-shirts made and the placards printed.

Sabina had had no idea that staging a protest took such planning. She could only hope her agent didn't have her scheduled for any races on Wednesday. An entirely selfish thought. She was not cut out for the role of martyr.

"How long do you figure we'll be out on strike?" asked one of the exercise riders.

"As long as it takes to bring them around," said Charlotte.

"Wait a minute," Bonnie drawled. "Some of us got kids to feed. Count me in for one day. That's it. It's all I can afford."

"We've all got money problems," said Patsy. "That's the crux of this whole matter. But if we're going to get anywhere, we're all going to have to sacrifice."

Exactly how much sacrifice would be required of her, Sabina didn't realize until she got home and took the messages off her answering machine. Her agent had called to tell her that Bardy Mulligan wanted her to ride Xenophon in the eighth race on Wednesday.

For the first time her blue chair seemed to be smirking instead of smiling. She drove an angry fist into it, but the smirk remained.

Was there a way she could get out of the strike? As the only woman jockey, it would turn the protest into a joke.

She could just see the TV reporters asking, "And where is the only woman jockey at San Felipe?"

"Sorry, she's unavailable right now. She's out on the track riding in a high-stakes race."

"Then what the hell are you girls complaining about?"

But this was her chance to ride Xenophon. He was a horse any jockey at San Felipe would want to ride. How could she pass him up?

That was looking at it selfishly. After all, if it hadn't been for Miguel Carrasco, she would not have been offered the horse. Before he'd spoken to Bardy, the only trainer with enough guts to let her ride had been Frank. And no matter how well she rode, even now, few of them would be bending over backward to give another woman a chance. Maybe the publicity would work. It had helped other groups break down barriers. And heaven knew, women jockeys needed the help as much as any deserving group.

Whatever she thought about Patsy and her methods of persuasion, it was still quite a coup to have gotten Miguel on their side. In fact, it was rather altruistic of Patsy. She herself had not thought of using Miguel to further the worthy cause of women jockeys.

The phone rang. She hoped it was Miguel so that she wouldn't have to call him herself. It was getting impossible to put it off any longer.

But it was Patsy. "Hi, you rushed off before I could talk to you. Can you believe that about Carrasco? I was dying to tell you this morning. I just couldn't believe his turnaround! I'd always heard all these terrible things about chauvinistic Latin men. It just goes to show, you can't stereotype people. Of course, there's also the stereotype of the Latin lover, and . . ."

Sabina ground her teeth together to keep from screaming an obscenity into the receiver. "Look, Patsy, I'm right in the middle of something." Right in the middle of holding myself together, she thought.

"Okay, but I have so much to tell you."

"Patsy," said Sabina tersely, "I know this may shock you, but I have absolutely no desire to hear all the gory details. Save the play by plays for someone else."

"Sure." Patsy sounded deflated. "You're still teaching the class tomorrow afternoon, aren't you?"

"Yes, one o'clock, same place."

"Good, because I told Miguel, and he's going to be there. He really is such a sweetheart. You won't believe what he . . ."

"I've really got to be going, Patsy." That obscenity was balancing dangerously on the tip of her tongue. "Talk to you tomorrow."

No sooner did the receiver hit the cradle and the obscenity erupt, but the phone rang again. She picked it up and barked out an angry "Hello." Then, realizing who it was, she softened. "Oh, hi, Mom."

"Are you okay?" her mother asked with concern. It was hard to hide a depressed mood from one's mother.

"Just tired."

"You work too hard," admonished her mother. "Are you racing tomorrow afternoon?"

"No, just exercising in the morning, then I teach that class again in Griffith Park. I thought I'd stop by afterward. Maybe Dad and I can take a ride."

"But, honey, you ride every day for a living. I'd think you'd want to relax a little." Her mother, who had always been terrified of horses, had never reconciled herself to the love her husband and daughter lavished on the creatures.

"But that's riding for work," Sabina explained. "I miss riding for pleasure, just getting up in the hills and forgetting about everything."

"You'll stay for dinner?" asked her mother hopefully. "I was so sorry we had to cancel the other night. San Francisco was miserable and rainy."

"I'd love dinner, Mom, but don't make any pies or anything."

"Sabina, you're all skin and bones!"

"I've got to keep my weight down, Mom."

There was a motherly sigh at the other end of the phone. "I know, I know. Listen, honey, there's a couple at our church we met the other night, and . . ."

"And they have a son," Sabina finished for her.

"Now, don't cut me off until I tell you about him. He's a lawyer and . . ."

"Mom, I appreciate what you want to do, but I'm just not interested in getting involved with anyone right now."

"I'm just afraid that when you do, it will be another one of those good-for-nothing jockeys."

Sabina had never told her mother about Al's death. When she was seven, and her best friend broke her leg from a fall off a horse, she hadn't told her mother that, either. She had the kind of mother who worried about everything from aphid infestation on her roses to the effects of nuclear war on Burbank.

But most of all she worried about her daughter riding racehorses for a living. Sabina knew that every time her mother read about a jockey being injured or killed, another hair turned gray. Fortunately for her mother's precarious peace of mind, Al's death had been inconsequential enough to miss the California papers. Instead of telling her mother, she had explained his absence by saying he'd run off and married another woman.

Another maternal sigh came through the telephone lines. "All right, honey. No young lawyer. No pies. We'll barbeque chicken. How's that?"

"Great, Mom. See you then."

She stared at the telephone for a moment after she hung up. Unbidden, the little gremlins in their jockey silks marched into her consciousness again. As a mother, not a jockey, would she worry about them racing? Unwelcome little brats! Why didn't they leave her alone?

She turned on her answering machine in case Miguel called and went to bed. It was cowardly not to call him, but after that last conversation with Patsy, she simply wasn't up to it. The phone rang several times that night, and when she checked the recorder the next morning, she found the messages had all been from Miguel.

She dreaded having to face him together with Patsy in the class that afternoon. When she arrived at the rental stable, he was at the center of a tight knot of her students. She recognized the look in their eyes, the awe mixed with enchantment. Any jockey of his caliber would have inspired the awe of a group of aspiring jockeys, but only Miguel Carrasco managed to make their feminine hearts flutter as well.

Patsy wasn't with the rest of the group. The organizer, she was picking the horses they were going to ride, getting them ready for the class.

The moment Miguel saw Sabina, he broke away from the girls and came toward her. Putting an arm around her, he led her away from the others. "You never called me last night," he said quietly. "Why?"

"I got in late."

"That wouldn't have mattered. Something is bothering you. Why are you afraid to tell me?"

"I'm not afraid!"

"Then?"

She looked nervously at the students, who were monitoring their every move. "Let's talk after class."

He nodded and turned on his heel. "All right, what's the matter with you lazy people?" he said to the girls. "Why aren't you all like Patsy, saddling those horses? You want to be jockeys? You must know more than how to ride a horse."

In spite of her anger at him, she couldn't help smiling at the way he handled them. He made sure each one of them knew everything there was to know about a racing saddle and bridle before they mounted.

Since it was an unstructured class, both of them critiqued the riding, working well as a team, putting their personal tension aside for the moment in an effort to help the riders. Sabina was surprised to find out how much she herself was learning from Miguel. He was explaining basics she hadn't thought about in years.

When the horses began to tire, Miguel asked each of them to bring their horses to a halt as he surveyed the way they were sitting and how their hands were placed. Sabina felt a painful twinge when she saw him take Patsy's leg and turn her knee in. Turn her knee in? Patsy had never had that trouble before. The girl was shameless. Patsy flashed Miguel a grateful smile.

After the class was over, the girls all wanted to treat their instructors to coffee, but Sabina declined and so did Miguel. "Where can we go talk?" he asked her, taking her aside.

"Why don't you go have coffee with them?" asked Sabina. "I told my mother I'd be over this afternoon to see her. My parents live right by here."

"Then I'll go with you. I'd like to meet them."

"Miguel. . . ." She couldn't foist another jockey off on her mother, not after the conversation yesterday.

"We have to talk, Sabina. I am not going to let this go on. You mean too much to me."

She saw Patsy watching them, her eyes filled with jealousy. First Natasha, then her, now Patsy . . . was any man worth all this pain?

He followed her the few blocks to her parents' home in his own car. The neighborhood was a far cry from the exclusive one where Miguel lived. Sabina had grown up in a solid, middle-class suburb of tree-lined streets, ranch-style homes with shutters, brick walkways, trimmed lawns and pampered rose bushes.

Sabina liked coming home. Nothing ever changed from year to year. There was a comforting stability about it all. Nobody ever used front doors or formal living rooms. Back doors were unlocked and led into comfortable family rooms or kitchens.

Her mother, as usual, was sitting at the kitchen table, drinking coffee and talking on the phone. She looked up, surprised to see someone with Sabina.

She hugged her mother and introduced her to Miguel. "We were teaching the class together this afternoon," she said to explain his presence.

Her father came through the door wearing jeans and boots. "Miguel Carrasco!" He crossed the room to shake the younger man's hand. "What a pleasure to have you here. I have been an admirer of yours for years. You'll stay for dinner, won't you?"

"I would be very honored," said Miguel.

It was too late to shoot a warning glance at her father. Her mother was already frowning.

"I wanted to be a jockey when I was a kid," her father was saying, "but I got too big. Guess Sabina picked up all my ambitions."

After a brief attempt at being a trainer, her father had done stunt riding for the studios until the movie Western all but became extinct. By then he had broken enough bones to be convinced by his wife to go into something tamer. He became a film lighting technician, but never lost his love for horses.

"Come on out back," he said to Miguel. "See what you think of my thoroughbreds. I bought 'em both off the track about ten years ago. There's no horse worth a damn, in my opinion, but a thoroughbred."

"You have horses in your backyard?" asked Miguel with surprise as he followed her father out the back door.

"We've got our stables attached to the garage. Burbank has special zoning for it. You only have to be eighteen feet from the house. Makes this the only sensible place to live in Los Angeles county, in my opinion. Of course the studios are all around here. People talk about Hollywood, but what they really mean is Burbank. Nothing going on in Hollywood. It's just the name, I guess."

"This is a wonderful setup," said Miguel, looking at the elaborate barn and corrals.

"Dad built the whole thing from scratch," said Sabina proudly.

"My wife is always complaining I never do anything around the house. Well, truth is, this is where I like to spend my leisure time."

"Your wife doesn't ride?" asked Miguel.

He shook his head. "Scared to death of horses. I didn't want my kid to be scared of 'em, so I started taking Sabina out when she was about six months old. Her mother had a fit, but Sabina loved it. Cried when I took her down. I had a big Western saddle and just stuck her in front. She held onto the horn. Not scared of anything. At three years old she was demanding to handle a horse all by herself, no lead rope or anything."

"Your Sabina is quite a rider," said Miguel.

Her father's eyes lit up. "You think so? She's had a rough time getting mounts at San Felipe."

"She's going to do well," said Miguel with confidence.

She left the two men talking about thoroughbreds and went back inside to see her mother. It was not surprising that her father and Miguel were getting along so well. Horse people generally did. Even the people who were as driven to succeed as Miguel had a calm, easy-going way about them. Frantic personalities were never effective around a horse.

"A jockey, eh?" was her mother's comment as she loaded the dishwasher. "Too good-looking, that one, Sabina. That's the kind of man women kill each other over. You don't need that kind of trouble."

Sabina helped herself to a cup of coffee. "I agree with you."

"You do?" Her mother looked at her with

surprise. "You never agree with me. Are you feeling well?"

Sabina laughed. "Maybe I'm growing up."

"My prayers are being answered. Are you sure you wouldn't like to meet that nice lawyer?"

"Not *that* grown-up, Mom. Now, tell me, what's the good gossip around the neighborhood."

While her mother was filling her in on all the latest marriages, divorces and babies, Miguel and her father came back in.

"No, you and Sabina take the horses out," her father was saying.

"But you had planned to ride together," protested Miguel.

"You're not going riding, Dad?" asked Sabina. She wasn't sure exactly how it had transpired that she was suddenly going riding with Miguel. It would be impossible now to avoid the unpleasant confrontation. And what she feared most was a confession that he had made love to Patsy.

"You two go," her father insisted. "Miguel's never ridden in Griffith Park. Take him up top to the Observatory. It's so clear this time of year, you should be able to see all the way out to the ocean."

"What about your ankle?" she asked Miguel.

"It's fine as long as I don't put pressure on it. I'll ride bareback."

"Go ahead," urged her father. "You'd be doing me a favor. How often does a guy get to say Miguel Carrasco rode one of his horses?"

Before she knew it, she was riding down the street with Miguel beside her. "I like this area very much," he said as he gazed around at the houses. "Had I known there was a place like this so close to the track, I would have moved here instead of San Felipe."

"And give up your estate?"

"Having a horse in the backyard would be wonderful."

"Living in San Felipe is like having several hundred horses in your backyard," noted Sabina. "It's not as if you never get a chance to ride."

"But not like this. Just for pleasure. It takes me back to being a boy again. My father was like yours. He loved his horses."

"They're like his kids. Some men come home after work, have a cocktail and turn on the TV. Dad comes home, brushes his horses and takes off for the hills. He'll ride one for a while, and pony the other, then change off. I used to rush to finish my homework at night so I could ride with him."

"At night?"

"That's the best time in Griffith Park. Spooky, too. These hills are full of legends. I'll show you the cliff where the Doña Los Feliz threw herself off when she had been betrayed. When you pass by there at night, you get goose bumps and the hackles rise on the back of your neck. Of course, that's where my father always told me ghost stories. One Halloween we all organized a ride and had people dressed up as ghosts and goblins along the trails. It was wonderful."

They went through the equestrian tunnels that took them under the Ventura Freeway and onto the riding trails. "Only in Los Angeles would you have to go under a freeway to get to a riding trail," laughed Miguel.

"The people in our neighborhood fought for that access when the freeway was built. They would have laid themselves in front of freeway traffic to be assured of their trails."

She took him through winding Oak Canyon and up a steep incline. "We named this trail Suicide. This is the real test for bareback riders. Now I'll see how good a rider you really are. If you can keep from sliding off going up here, you're okay."

Sabina wasn't really worried about him. Miguel was as natural on a horse bareback as he was on a racing saddle. Riding bareback, with legs gripping the sides of the horse, was actually safer than being perched up above in the precarious racing position.

They followed the trail, reaching the top of the hill without mishap. The longer they rode through the lush green winter foliage, the better she felt and the less she wanted to despise Miguel.

Being with him like this was sheer pleasure. As a teenager, growing up here, she used to wish she had a boyfriend to ride in the hills with. But her boyfriends had been interested in other sports. Even with Al, she had never gone riding just for the fun of it. For him riding had been work, and when he was off the track, he'd put horses out of his mind.

Miguel was enjoying the ride immensely, stopping to comment on wildflowers and trees, marveling at the scenery as it unfolded. She was delighted to find that they felt the same sense of tranquility in the open.

At the top of the ridge they stopped to look out over the hills. It was a cloudless day, and the hills were carpeted emerald green from the rain. Bright golden poppies and yellow mustard were beginning to crop up. Oak trees were covered with fresh new foliage.

In silent agreement she and Miguel slid off their horses and walked.

"This reminds me of home," said Miguel with a smile as he looked around. "I had forgotten how it was to be with a horse, feel the earth crunch beneath your feet."

"I used to like to go barefoot out here. My dad would have killed me if he'd known, with all the rattlesnakes."

Two deer darted across the trail and up the hillside. "Late summer you see them down around the golf course," she said. "It gets pretty dry up here. At night the coyotes come out. They have a field day down in the picnic areas on the weekends."

Miguel was watching her. Her brown hair was loose and blowing in the breeze. "You are more beautiful than ever out here," he said. "If I were never to see you again, this is the way I would best like to remember you."

"Better than on the satin sheets?" She didn't know what prompted her to say that. It was bound to provoke the very subject she wanted to avoid.

Miguel broke off a pink wildflower and placed it in her hair. "That is a difficult choice. You were very beautiful with your dark hair fanned out on the satin pillows. But I would like to see your hair spread out on the grass amongst the wildflowers. There is that look again, an accusing look. What are you accusing me of?"

One word would suffice. "Patsy."

His dark eyes narrowed. "Did she tell you that we made love the other morning?" he asked suspiciously.

"Not exactly, but she gave me an amazingly accurate description of the Jacuzzi and your bedroom."

"She expressed an interest in seeing the house, so I took her on a tour."

"That's all?"

"Damn it, Sabina. I wouldn't lie to you. The only reason I wanted to talk to Patsy at all was because of you."

"What does Patsy Dimpton have to do with me?"

"Ever since we all had coffee that morning, she's been after me to make a commitment to support the all-women race. My first inclination was to support it if it would help you, but I wasn't sure that was the best motivation for taking a stand. Because I am who I am, what I say will influence people. And it seemed to me that if I wanted to help you, I could do much better for you on a personal level. This was an issue that would involve the media and San Felipe Meadows as well. I wanted to hear what Patsy had to say, and there was never much time at the track, so I invited her to breakfast. I fed her breakfast, took her on a tour of the house, listened to her arguments, made up my mind, and then she left. That's all there was to it."

Sabina gazed at him suspiciously. "You want me to believe that you didn't notice her rather obvious little come ons?"

"If they had been directed exclusively at me, I

might have taken them seriously, but as you well know, Patsy takes aim at many targets."

"You're using a double standard," Sabina noted. "Why do men think they're the only ones who can be the conquistadors?"

"Now you are defending Patsy? What a contradictory woman you are, Sabina." He cupped a hand around her neck as they walked. "The first night we are together you want to throw me at Natasha, and now you accuse me of using a double standard because I did not let Patsy seduce me. You are so eager to see me with other women that I am beginning to wonder if you care for me at all."

"You really didn't do anything with Patsy the other morning?"

"I had breakfast with her. For God's sake, Sabina, I am so in love with you I can't see straight. When I saw Patsy you and I had just had the most extraordinary night of love I have ever had in my life."

He wrapped his arms around her and drew her tightly into them. "Sabina, don't ever put me through this again," he growled. "Don't ever doubt my love."

They kissed, and she was filled with his love and her own need for him.

Not wanting to relinquish the physical contact, he slipped an arm around her shoulders and they continued walking the horses. Part of the trail had been washed away by the rains, so she took him down a narrow deer path. "This is a shortcut down to the Observatory."

It had been several years since she'd taken the trail. It had become overgrown with low-hanging oak branches and prickly toyon bushes filled with red berries.

"I can't say much for your shortcuts," Miguel called down to her.

They reached a small clearing, and she glanced around for the path. "I think it used to be over there, but . . ." The oat grass was four feet high in places. It was impossible to see where the path was.

Miguel took her in his arms. "You're lying. You just lured me into this secluded place to seduce me."

She wriggled out of his grasp. "What an ego. You think all women are out to seduce you."

Miguel laughed and took the reins from her hand. He tied the two horses to a tree where they could nibble on the green wild oats.

She could not help thinking that Miguel, wearing faded jeans that clung to his strongly muscled legs, was more attractive than she'd ever seen him. Everything around them, the plants, the fragrances, seemed to be reawakening. Spring was about to begin, kindling something elemental and primitive in her depths.

Chapter 10

THE GRASS WAS SPRINGY AND COOL BENEATH THEM.
As he had promised, Miguel fanned out her long
dark hair and entwined it with wild mustard
blossoms.

"Don't ever be worried about another woman,
Sabina," he said softly. "It's you I love. More
than I can possibly tell you."

Wildflower soft kisses grazed her forehead, her
cheeks, her neck and, as her blouse opened, her
breasts. As she watched his lips pull at the dark
tips, she marveled at the beautiful, rugged planes
of his face, the straight slash of dark eyebrows and
long lashes. Her mother was right. In less-
civilized times he would have been a man women
would kill each other to have.

She ran her hands up under his shirt and over
the hard muscles of his shoulders and back. Each

curve of flesh seeming more exciting than the next.

How strange and wonderful it was to be loved by him. It was as though everything in her life had been leading to him, to this moment in the hills she loved, with the horses nearby.

She wrapped her arms around him tightly as they kissed. They rolled around in the grass so that she was above him. Wanting to show him how much she loved him, she found his male nipples hidden in the dark chest hair and drew them hard.

As her lips moved lower her long hair, entwined with the mustard flowers, fell over his chest like a silken scarf, and she heard him moan with pleasure, wrapping his fingers in its folds.

She loved the texture of his skin, the taste, the feel of it under the palms of her hands as she caressed the ridges and valleys of his strong body. She lost herself in him, in loving him. Giving him pleasure was all that mattered, enveloping him in the beauty of her love.

But he twisted below her and, imprisoning her hips, began to return the pleasure. Sabina gasped. Shafts of prismatic light seemed to shoot through her as they moved into new, beguiling configurations of loving.

When at last she felt him enter her, she found herself responding with provocative rhythms and movements she had not known she'd possessed.

His fingers swept across her tingling skin. With each thrust of his love they flew closer to the blazing sun, until wings melting, they plunged with breathtaking speed into the soft, green, wildflower-strewn bower beneath them.

"Sabina, we belong together," he said as he held her to him. She rested her head on his chest. One of the horses had pulled loose from his tether and was nibbling on the grass around them. Miguel ran a hand over the horse's soft nose. "We'll get a ranch and raise thoroughbreds. Put a house on it for your parents when your dad retires. He'd like that, raising thoroughbreds. You've still got a few years to race. Good years. So we'll . . ."

She lifted her head to look at him. "Am I hearing this right?"

He pulled her head down and kissed her. "Yes, you are, *mi amor*. I want you forever."

"Marriage?" she whispered incredulously.

"Marriage, little children in jockey suits, if you'd like," he said with a laugh. "Ever since you mentioned that the other night, I've been thinking about them, as though they already existed. It's very strange, Sabina. I have never thought about having children with any woman before."

"I thought about them too. You wouldn't expect me to give up racing once I had them, would you?" she asked cautiously. "I know this mother and daughter in the Midwest who race against each other. In fact, wouldn't it be fun, Miguel, if we all raced together? They could start a new slogan, the family that races together . . ."

He put his fingers to her lips. "No, Sabina, I'm going to retire."

She ran her fingers through his thick dark hair. His words came as a shock. They were words she had never thought she'd hear from him.

"When there was nothing in my life but racing, I could not leave it. It held the memories, the loneliness, at bay. But you give my life another meaning. For the first time there is something that means more to me than winning races. I realized that this afternoon, riding with you up here. I could never give up riding entirely. Horses are a part of me. I want to share that with you and our children—like this, riding free in the hills for the pure pleasure of it. And I want you to continue to race as long as you love it. In fact, I'll raise and train horses for you to take into the winners' circle. We'll have a good life, Sabina."

"Miguel, I love you so much." She covered his face with kisses. "And I want so badly to make you happy."

He lifted her face and grinned at her. "That you do, but enough of this for now. It's getting late, and your parents will worry about us if we're not back."

He gave her a leg up, then took his horse's mane and vaulted on. After finding the narrow path again, they followed it down the hill and came to the main trail. "We'll save the Observatory for another day," she told him. "There's a quicker way home along the golf course."

The sun was beginning its descent, and the long shadows brought the crickets into concert. They were on a long flat stretch of trail, riding beneath scented pine trees, when the horses, knowing how close they were to home, broke into a canter.

Being thoroughbreds, each one tried to pull ahead of the other. Sabina and Miguel laughed as they kept the horses to a lope. Then the competitive spirit got hold of her. She let her horse out slightly, passing Miguel.

He did not let her get ahead for long, and the

minute he shot ahead, her horse strained against the bit to catch up.

Before they knew it, the pace had increased until they were at a full gallop, dodging low-hanging branches and racing toward the hill. She pulled her knees up and leaned low over the horse's neck, urging him forward.

Miguel was doing the same. She had never seen anything so superb as Miguel riding bareback. He leaned low over the horse's neck, the mane and tail of the thoroughbred streaking out behind him in the wind.

She wished her father could see them. He had bought both horses cheaply off the track because their owners didn't think they had much speed, but he'd always thought they just hadn't been trained properly. It would be a thrill for him to watch Miguel Carrasco on his horse.

When they reached the hill and felt the horses heating up, they pulled them up and walked them to cool them off. Miguel patted his horse's neck and blew Sabina a kiss.

"I changed my mind," he said to her. "Racing is still damn fun."

"You're not going to retire now?" In a way she was glad. Miguel was too fine a jockey to give the sport up now. There was always the possibility of breaking bones, of course. But Miguel was in magnificent physical shape. He had years and years of racing left in him. There was no reason he couldn't become another Johnny Longden.

"Just one more race," he said. "I don't want my last race to be remembered as the one where I hit the dirt. I'm going to ride Composure in the

San Felipe Derby, and I'm going to win. Go out in style."

"Wait a minute, Miguel. Any horse but Composure! Next time he'll kill you! You're out of your mind. That's just macho nonsense. Ride in the Derby. Ride in a hundred more races, but leave Composure out of it. One of the jockeys after that last race said that the only thing that horse is good for is dog food."

"No. The Derby on Composure. That horse has the speed to win it. And in spite of that accident, I like him. He's had some bad handling, that's the only problem with him. I'm going to go out there every day from now until the Derby and work with him, take him in and out of the starting gate so many times he'll think it's carrot heaven."

"Miguel, why not ride Xenophon in the San Felipe Derby? For my money he's a much better horse than Composure, without all the psychological hangups."

Miguel grinned at her. "Because, my darling, you're going to ride Xenophon in the Derby."

"*Me* on Xenophon?"

"Bardy told me this morning. Depending, of course, on how you do next Wednesday. And I know you're going to do well."

She wanted to die. Wednesday was the day of the protest. Not only was she going to blow her chance to ride Xenophon, but her chance to ride in San Felipe's most prestigious race, where the purse money would be upwards of $500,000. Winning would give her ten percent of that, and it would finally establish her as a name jockey.

Quickly she explained to Miguel about the protest.

"Have them switch it to another day," he suggested.

"I'll try, but they've got press people coming out and everything."

He reached over and took her hand as they rode side by side. "I just had a beautiful inspiration. Why don't we get married the night after the Derby?"

"It's a wonderful idea," she said, "but I want my groom in one piece. Damn, but I wish you'd give up this nonsense of riding Composure!"

When they arrived back at her parent's house, it was already dark out. She and Miguel brushed the horses and put them back in their stalls. Her father had started up the barbeque. He fixed Miguel a drink, and the two of them stayed outside and talked horses while Sabina went inside to help her mother with the rest of the dinner.

"Have a good ride?" her mother asked casually as she washed her hands.

Sabina immediately thought of their spontaneous lovemaking and flushed. "Yes. Miguel really enjoyed Griffith Park."

"You're serious about him, aren't you?" asked her mother suddenly.

"I . . . I'm going to marry him," she blurted out.

"That was a quick turnaround from this afternoon," her mother noted wisely.

"I've fallen in love with him."

"The man's fast off the track as well as on, I see."

Sabina laughed. "No, it's been building for a while. It didn't just happen this afternoon."

"You're sure there's not a little hero worship acting there?"

"A lot of hero worship," Sabina admitted. "He's the most extraordinary man I've ever known. I think you'll agree once you get to know him."

"Your father thinks a lot of him." She gave her daughter a hug. "And that says quite a bit. Now, go slice some tomatoes for the salad and tell me about the wedding plans. You're not going to do something crazy like get married at the track, are you?"

She laughed. "No, we'll do it traditionally, but right after the San Felipe Derby."

"When's that?"

"In about a month."

Her mother frowned. "Not much time to plan anything elaborate. I suppose he would want something elaborate, wouldn't he? I mean the people he hangs out with. You just about have to invite their secret-service people to the wedding too." She glanced nervously around the combination kitchen-family room. "You don't think he'll mind eating in here tonight, do you? I can always put a tablecloth on the dining room table and bring out the good silver, though I think it needs polishing."

"Don't be silly. Miguel will love this."

Privately she wasn't so sure, knowing how he enjoyed the elegant luxuries of wealth, but he fit in beautifully. If her mother had had any reservations about Miguel, they were quickly erased during dinner. Mrs. Martin even gave him a hug at the door.

* * *

Miguel returned with Sabina to her apartment that night. Seeing her scrapbooks, he picked them up and began going through them page by page, asking questions about each photo. It made her feel good to know that he had the same curiosity about her childhood and past that she'd had about his. Being with her family had opened him up, and he began to talk more freely about his own, sharing memories that she knew he had kept locked up inside him until then.

"We were a very close family," he told her. "Because I was the youngest, my brothers sometimes used to give me a hard time, and we fought like crazy, but we were all very close. I still miss them. I think that is one reason I have enjoyed this kind of life. There is the same camaraderie with the jockeys as with members of a family."

"I always wanted brothers and sisters," she confessed. "I envied the neighborhood kids who had them, especially those from really big families. It was like they belonged to a secret club that I could never join."

"But it must have been wonderful growing up in a neighborhood like yours."

"If you liked horses, it was a dream. I always thought it was funny how in some families, even when the parents had horses and the kids were raised around them, some took to it and others didn't."

"I am surprised you didn't pick up any of your mother's fear."

"It was and is totally incomprehensible to me. To me horses were always big, lovable pets. Only once did my mother ever go into the corral, and that was when I was a toddler. I had managed to open the gate and was having a wonderful time, walking in and out between the horses' legs. It never occurred to me that those huge hoofs could flatten me out."

He chuckled. "My mother adored horses," he said fondly. "And she was quite a rider. I remember her racing against us, even helping round up cattle. My father was a superb horseman. He had a passion for thoroughbreds. Your father reminds me of him in that way. The family fortune was in cattle, but his pride was his horses. I can remember once, and I must have been very young at the time, when his prize stallion died. He sat down in the barn and wept."

Sabina learned that Miguel had been modest in his description of his family, which had been immensely wealthy. It was an old, landed family that traced its ancestry back to the original conquistadors from Spain.

"I'd like to have a lot of children," she said.

"So would I. Would you like to start making some tonight?" He gave her a devilish grin and pulled her onto his lap.

Their kiss was rudely interrupted by the ringing of the telephone. It was Charlotte Ficus, who wanted to discuss the plans for the protest.

Sabina gazed across the room at Miguel sitting in her smiling blue chair. For the moment she didn't want to think of anything but him.

"We've called the press conference for noon so that we'll have the maximum number of people out there. I'm going to speak first, then I'm going to hand the mike over to you to answer questions."

"Listen, Charlotte," she began hesitantly. "My

agent's got me booked on one of the best horses at San Felipe on Wednesday and if I do well on him, I've got a shot to ride in the San Felipe Derby. Is there any way we can change the date of the protest?"

"I had a feeling you'd back out when it got down to the wire," said Charlotte sarcastically.

"You can't move the date to Thursday?"

"No chance. I've already called all the TV stations and sent the press releases out. It would throw everything off kilter to shift things around now. Every one of the networks is going to be out there and all the local TV stations. Plus the newspapers. They loved the story, and they all wanted to do interviews with you, Sabina. You can race if you want to, but it's going to make us all look damn silly. All the girls are giving up their exercising fees that morning by walking out. I don't know why you can't give up a mount."

Sabina tried to put Xenophon out of her mind. She thought about what the others were sacrificing—for her, really. They were doing it to promote women jockeys. She thought about her friends who could be coming out to race at San Felipe and what the publicity could do for the plight of women jockeys in general.

Then she thought about that beautiful brown colt, the way he'd felt striding out under her that morning.

"You may never forgive me for this, Charlotte, but Wednesday I'm going to ride in that race. If you want to switch the date to Thursday, I'll be there." There was a rush of guilt as the last word came out, but there was no other way she could have answered. Racing came before anything else.

There was a brief silence at the other end of the line. "I'll switch it," said Charlotte quietly. "But damn it, Sabina, you'd just better place in that race."

"I'll give it my best," said Sabina with relief.

"I should be blazing mad at you, but it occurs to me that your winning the race, if you do, could be the best publicity of all. We could go out there and say, 'Look, fellows, here's a woman jockey who can finish in the money on a top horse. Let's give more of 'em a chance.'"

Miguel looked up from the scrapbooks as she hung up the phone. "Did she switch the date?"

Sabina nodded. "For a moment there I really didn't think she would."

"Those women need you more than you need them," he said. "Charlotte knows that. Don't let them get you involved if you don't want to be."

"I'm more than willing to help out," said Sabina. "God knows, women in this business need all the help they can get. But when it came down to a choice between riding Xenophon and walking around with a picket sign, there was no contest."

"And what happens if you're scheduled for a horse Thursday?" he asked.

She groaned. "For the first time in my life, I'm hoping I don't get a mount. No, that's not true. I do want a mount. I just might ride. Do you think I'm a rotten, selfish bitch?"

"You're a jockey. Any jockey would do the same in your situation."

"What do you think they'll ask me at the press conference?"

"They'll want to know how much trouble you've had at San Felipe."

"I'm getting butterflies in my stomach just thinking about it. I used to get stage fright when I had to give a book report in school. I hate talking in front of a lot of people. I'm fine on a horse. Do you think I could do the press conference from the back of a horse?"

Miguel put the scrapbooks down and pulled her onto his lap. "You'll do fine, my love. Don't worry about it. Would you like me to be there?"

"That would be lovely. You could hold my hand and give me courage," she said, kissing him.

"I shall hold your hand and announce our engagement."

She traced a loving line over his bottom lip. "I'm afraid it would turn out to be a very, very short engagement."

"Why?"

"Charlotte would kill us both right there on the spot for taking the women out of the limelight."

Miguel bit down lightly on her fingertip. "That is true, and what's more, it would seem as though I were helping the women just because of you, not because I believed in the cause. Under the circumstances, I think we should delay announcing our engagement until after this is settled."

"Do you really think the San Felipe officials will change their minds about the all-women race?"

"If there's enough public pressure brought to bear on them. It is worth giving it a try."

"Do you think the trainers will resent my being involved in this, Miguel?"

"Would that stop you?"

"No," she said quickly. "The only thing that would stop me from being there is getting another mount like Xenophon. And there aren't many like him."

"Except Composure," he reminded her with a grin. "But think realistically, Sabina. Your being involved in that protest might anger some of them. Probably not Bardy. As long as you were bringing his horses in on the money, he wouldn't care if you painted yourself blue, but with some of the others, you're taking a chance. Are you willing to risk it?"

She snuggled up against him, resting her head on his shoulder. "If worst comes to worst, there's always selling Racing Forms."

Chapter 11

LIVING WITH MIGUEL CARRASCO WAS GOING TO BE physically demanding, Sabina soon learned. He did not believe in keeping his weight down by mere dieting. The Olympic-size pool was for more than looks. He swam five miles every day, did fifty push-ups and bicycled two miles. And he insisted that she keep up with him.

"If you want to be in the winners' circle on Wednesday," he told her, "you are going to have to be in as good a shape as the rest of them. McDonald does a hundred push-ups every day. Lopez runs six miles."

"I'm going to be too exhausted to race Wednesday," she complained breathlessly as she finished another lap.

"One more lap and you'll have done a mile. That's enough for today. You can work up gradually."

Nothing she could say would dissuade him from going ahead with his plan to ride Composure in the Derby. He was at the track every morning at six, working exclusively with the horse. Normally a racehorse was taken out, galloped around the track a few times, hot-walked until he was cool, then put back in his stall. Miguel, however, was spending the entire morning with Composure.

Since he was still unable to put much pressure on his ankle, he rode with the stirrups longer than normal and with leather leggings to protect the ankle. Much of his time was spent walking Composure around the barn area and the paddock, circling him around the starting gate, taking him in and out of it. Out on the track he began the horse at an easy lope, learning which places frightened him. He brought the horse up to the trouble spots again and again until the animal no longer shied at them.

Sabina's heart stood still every time she saw the horse misbehave. But nothing she or any of his friends could say would stop Miguel. The same discipline and determination that had driven him to the top was driving him to make this horse into a champion. His last champion.

The one thing she could be thankful for was that Miguel was getting a chance to try his hand at training. She knew he would never be happy off the track. He needed the stimulation and challenge. His skill and knowledge of horses could make him one of the most successful trainers in the world.

One morning she found herself at the starting gate ready to breeze a horse for Frank when

Miguel placed Composure into the chute next to her.

"I've got to hand it to you," she said as she watched the horse enter the chute calmly. "You really do have him believing this is carrot heaven."

"Before I'm through with him, I want him believing the finish line is carrot heaven."

As they broke from the gate she kept pace with him for the first quarter mile. Then he let Composure out. She could see why Miguel was lavishing attention on this horse. The speed and agility of the animal was breathtaking to watch.

There was no way Frank's horse could keep up with him. Xenophon would be another story.

By Wednesday, everyone at the track was talking about the women's protest. Several of the trainers were making derisive comments to the women and threatening to fire them if they did not show up for work that Thursday.

One exercise girl expressed sympathy with the cause, but explained that she was supporting herself and three children on the money. "We're talking food on the table for the kids," she said. "The only way I stay away from work is if I'm too sick to get out of bed, and that hasn't happened once in five years. But you can bet I'll be there at noon."

Sabina began to feel guilty about making Charlotte delay the entire protest to accommodate her Wednesday race. And although none of the trainers were threatening to take her off their horses, she had to field their sarcastic comments. Many of them could not understand why she had any reason to complain. "You're riding here, aren't you?" one of them scoffed.

Aside from Miguel, who had expressed his solidarity, the jockeys were curiously quiet on the subject. Sabina knew that if even a few of them opposed the all-women race, the threat of a lawsuit would be sufficient to make the San Felipe management stick by their original decision.

The morning of the race Sabina tried to put all these political considerations aside until the race was over.

Xenophon was wonderfully fit. Looking him over that morning, she was once again awed by his beauty.

Now that he knew her, he leaned his head far out of his stall so that she could scratch under his chin.

It was impossible to avoid thinking about the protest, however. Even in the jockey room, questions were being directed her way. She explained how afraid most women jockeys were of tackling a track like San Felipe, even when they'd done well elsewhere. It was in small discussions like this that she began to feel more comfortable with words, and realized that she might be able to handle a press conference after all.

Only jockeys who were scheduled to race were allowed in the jockey room. But Miguel was waiting in the paddock area with Bardy and accompanied her into the walking circle.

"Don't forget your damn goggles," said Miguel with a wink as she buckled her chin strap.

She grinned at him.

Bardy gave the horse another last-minute once

over and said to her, "Use your own judgment out there. You know this horse. Just give him some time to get himself together."

On the parade to post she tried to forget how much was depending on this race. The women needed her to win or at least place to make the protest credible, but most of all she needed a win to get into the Derby.

Someone shouted from the stands, "Go to it, Sabina, girl. I got my money on you."

Another party heard from. She'd almost forgotten all the bettors who were depending on her to bring Xenophon across the finish line ahead of the field. Two professional handicappers had made her their choice to win.

Xenophon walked into the starting gate. The door clanged shut and the noise frightened him. He snorted and threw his head in the air.

An assistant starter standing on the bars beside her reached out for the bridle to hold him.

"Take it easy with him," said Sabina. "He's a little spooky."

She grabbed a fistful of black mane and waited. The flag was up.

Xenophon reared up as the latch sprang, then came down hard and stumbled forward. Sabina let go of the mane and bounced to a crouch. She sat quietly, waiting for the colt to pull himself together. She hoped the clumsy start was not a forerunner of things to come. As Bardy had suggested, she let the colt relax and find his stride. She wouldn't rush him.

Coming around the turn she saw Rich Dempsey, an apprentice jockey, just ahead of her. She could see he was going to attempt to move into an impossible space between two horses. Paul McDonald yelled at him, "Hey, don't do that! Don't go in there, jock!"

It took experience to know when you had enough horse to move into a tight spot. Dempsey didn't make it. His horse clipped the heels of the horse in front, stumbled, but didn't go down.

Dempsey, however, was struggling desperately to stay on the horse. Sabina quickly moved up beside him and pulled him back up into the saddle.

"Thanks," he gasped as he regained his balance.

"You okay?"

"Yeah."

In helping Rich, however, she had lost ground. Her own weight shift as she pulled him up had thrown Xenophon off stride. She was still far behind, and the lead horses were already heading into the final stretch.

She turned her wrists, gathering Xenophon up. She tapped him on the shoulder with her stick, and he quickly responded. He was still more horse than any out there, she knew.

The same space Dempsey had tried to push into had opened up again, this time with enough room for her mount. Xenophon charged through the two horses and moved into the clear, striding out like he never had before. Knees locked in and arm swinging with the stick, she felt the rhythmic syncronization of their two bodies.

They passed the horse laying fourth, then third. Just a few more seconds, she prayed. Xenophon was giving her everything he had. He was only a half length behind the lead horse. But they were under the wire.

There wasn't much she could say to Bardy or Xenophon's owner as they came through the tunnel. They all knew that if she had not helped the apprentice jockey, she would have won the race by several lengths.

But neither of them brought it up. Rich Dempsey could have been killed. Any jockey that close to him would have helped out if he could. She remembered a time in Arizona when she had been in danger of going over. Two jockeys, one on either side, had helped her back up. In those crucial seconds when you saw another rider in trouble, you didn't stop to think that you might blow the race. You did what you could to help, then did your damedest to make up for it later.

Back in the jockey room Rich came up to thank her. With his sandy hair and large blue eyes, he looked even younger than his eighteen years, and somehow he reminded her of Al.

"Hey, thanks for helping me out," he said shyly. "I guess I should've listened to McDonald out there."

She shrugged. "Those things happen. I'm sure you'll return the favor some day."

Several of the jockeys also came up to her and thanked her for what she had done.

Outside the jockey room Bardy was talking to Xenophon's owner. He motioned her over. She held her breath, knowing they had been discussing the Derby.

"We've been talking it over," said Bardy.

"We'd like you to run Xenophon in the San Felipe Derby."

"Thanks . . . thank you very much," she said.

Miguel was waiting for her in the Turf Club. Excitedly she told him their decision.

"It doesn't surprise me," he said, and kissed her. His dark eyes were bright. "What a wedding day we are going to have!"

"Will you call off the wedding if I beat you out there?"

"Composure is not going to be beaten," he said with a grin.

"You want to bet?"

"All right. What shall we bet?"

She thought a moment. "If Xenophon wins, I'll be a very rich Senora Carrasco. I'll pay for the honeymoon."

"Ah, but there is no incentive for you to win if it will cost you money. You might throw the race. We must turn that around. The loser pays for the honeymoon."

"But if I lose, we won't be able to afford more than a weekend in a motel, and we'll both suffer."

"This is a very serious consideration," he said thoughtfully. "I know. I'll pay for the honeymoon if you lose, but you will owe me out of the money from the next Derby you win."

They shook hands on it and kissed again. Sabina noticed that some people were watching them. "We'd better keep this to ourselves until after tomorrow," she whispered.

When Sabina arrived at the track around eleven the next morning, she was surprised at how many women were there. Not all of them had stayed away from workouts earlier, but almost all of them were gathered outside the San Felipe gates to be part of the protest.

There were picket signs and banners. Many of them were wearing the green T-shirts Patsy had made up, which read, "Support Women Jockeys!"

Sabina had decided to dress conservatively in a tailored suit. Charlotte had wanted her to come decked out in jockey silks, but that, Sabina felt, was pushing "cute" to the extreme.

Miguel had said he would be there later, and she wished he would hurry. The butterflies in her stomach were increasing in direct proportion to the number of TV cameras that were being set up. Already some reporters were asking her questions.

The crowds arriving for the race stopped to gawk at the women, but the protest prevented few, if any, from going in. San Felipe was not likely to lose any money that afternoon.

Sabina was relieved to see Miguel finally arrive. Several reporters also spied him and quickly asked his opinion. "I am in favor of the race," he said. "I think there are some fine women jockeys and they should be given the chance to compete at San Felipe."

When the microphones were all set up, Charlotte went up to the podium and began speaking, giving statistics and describing the problems women had in breaking into all areas of the male-dominated sport. As she began to talk about the all-women race at San Felipe, she suddenly stopped in midsentence, and gazed wide-eyed at the racetrack entrance.

Sabina saw the cameras swing around as the crowd murmured. A dozen of San Felipe's top jockeys were coming toward them through the gate.

Paul McDonald, however, was the one who spoke for them all. "We just wanted to let the media know that all the jockeys who ride here took a vote last night, and we are all unanimously in favor of an all-women race. We have had the honor these past few months of riding against one of the finest jockeys in the country, who also happens to be a woman. We would like to see more riders like Sabina Martin competing out here."

Miguel told her later that her pulling Rich Dempsey back into the saddle had impressed them and influenced their votes.

The formal setting of the news conference quickly dissolved into a free for all. Reporters were grabbing anyone who would stand still long enough for an interview.

The jockeys who were scheduled for the first race returned to the jockey room, but some, including Rich Dempsey, stayed and faced the cameras.

Sabina had carefully prepared herself with statistics the night before, but she found to her surprise that most of the questions were being directed to Charlotte, while she was being pressed into making predictions about Xenophon's chances in the San Felipe Derby.

Patsy Dimpton, looking fetching in her body-tight green T-shirt, was telling anyone who would listen about her aspirations to become a jockey.

Miguel was being asked about Composure and if he really thought the horse had a chance in the Derby.

Bob Perile, looking as though the knot in his tie was too tight, tried to present San Felipe's point of view, but the unanimous vote of the jockeys had weakened his position considerably. Asked if he thought the San Felipe Board of Directors might reconsider their decision, he said yes.

After racing each other a mile in the pool, Sabina and Miguel went upstairs to his Jacuzzi and watched the newscasts on television.

"My nose looks long," she said after a moment. She was too mesmerized by how she looked to concentrate on what was being said.

"You look beautiful!" Miguel responded. "That's just the way the shadows are falling."

Slightly mollified, though suspicious of his defense, she listened for a moment, then groaned. "I keep saying 'uh' every two words, and 'you know.' I'm awful!"

"You are wonderful," he said. "But you're wrong about Xenophon. Composure will beat him."

She splashed some water on him and watched Miguel being interviewed. "You look like a movie star," she said after a moment, looking at him in person again. "San Felipe should fire the photographer who took your picture for the yearbook. You are extremely photogenic. That photo didn't do you justice. The number of jockey chasers is going to triple after they see this."

He switched stations and they watched themselves from different angles. "You see, there your nose looks every bit as lovely as it is." He emphasized his pronouncement by planting a kiss on her nose.

She had to admit her appearance had improved and suddenly understood why actresses were sensitive about being photographed from one side or the other.

This station ran a portion of her race on Xenophon the previous day. "Look at the way he tore up that field in the stretch! He made mincemeat out of those other horses. If Composure wants to beat him, he'll have to start out the night before."

"Did I tell you how Composure clocked out this morning?"

When she heard the number, the time did worry her slightly. "We'll see what he does in a race," she said. "Oh, there's Charlotte. She looks very good on camera."

Patsy appeared only briefly as the camera zoomed in on her T-shirt at the end of the piece.

Miguel floated Sabina onto his lap so that she faced him and pressed kisses on her throat. "You are going to get phone calls from cosmetic companies wanting you to push their products," he predicted. "Wasn't there a woman jockey a few years ago who did that?"

"That happens every few years. I guess the image sells perfume, though heaven knows why. Those of us who spend our life out there with the horses certainly don't smell like a French rose garden."

"Ah, but I told you, there is something very sexy about a woman on a fast horse."

His mouth found the tip of her breast. She moaned and dropped her head back into the swirling water, her long hair floating out behind her. His strong arms lifted her out of the water as his lips trailed down her skin.

There was no part of her now that he didn't know how to arouse. His thumbs pressed into the soft flesh where her thighs joined her hips and made erotic circles while he gently nibbled and licked.

Then he turned her so the Jacuzzi jets shot between her legs with a sensation so wildly alarming that she tried to move away from it.

"You don't like that?" he murmured with surprise.

The feeling was so intense that she could barely speak and told him with her eyes.

He laughed softly, moving her back against the stream of pulsing water. "I like to see your pleasure. It's like watching you on a racehorse."

"Sexy?" she asked breathlessly.

"Carrot heaven."

"Not yet, not without you," she said, and floated back to his arms, anchoring her legs around his back.

He was ready, thrusting powerfully into her, moving slowly so that they both felt the prisms of light flood them.

"I love you," she whispered, pulling him deeply into her.

"*Te quiero, mi amor,*" he said against her lips as their mouths opened to each other.

Love flowed through and around them until

Sabina wanted to cry, she was so filled with the emotion.

"Why don't you move in right away?" Miguel suggested reasonably as she lay in his arms later on the big brass bed.

She agreed. Any time away from him seemed an unneccesary deprivation.

Adjusting to living in more than two rooms and learning about life with servants, however, was not as easy as she had supposed. She was continually committing faux pas.

A towel was never hung back on the rack after being used, but left on the floor to be retrieved and washed.

One never made the bed in the morning, for the sheets were changed daily.

One did not dump a load of clothes in the washing machine. They were discreetly left in the hamper and the next day, they reappeared clean, ironed and folded.

If one was by the pool and hungry, one didn't meander back to the house and putter around in the kitchen. One picked up the pool phone and the desired snack arrived moments later, literally on a silver platter.

All things considered, however, she was certain that with some effort she could grow accustomed to the rigorous challenges of this kind of existence.

The morning after the press conference life at the track returned to normal. Threats to fire the exercise girls had been all bluster. And the issue of an all-women race took a back seat to the wonders of how everyone had looked on television.

Although Sabina expected some kind of statement from the San Felipe management in response to the protest, she couldn't find anyone who had heard anything concrete.

She was heading out to the training track on a one of Bardy's fillies when she saw Charlotte walking down to her barn. "You looked great on television last night," she called out to her.

"So'd you," said Charlotte with a grin. "We've got another meeting in Perile's office today at ten thirty. I think some press people are going to be there again, too. Oh, and by the way, can you exercise one of our fillies this morning?"

"Depends on what time. I'm booked until about nine forty-five."

"Then come on over at ten. We'll have her ready for you."

Her reputation as a solid rider was getting her almost more exercise mounts than she could handle. She was practically sprinting from barn to barn, jumping off one horse and getting on another. It was a good feeling.

Bob Perile's tie seemed even tighter this morning than usual. Sabina was surprised they were not offered coffee. Overnight their relationship with him had become overtly adversarial; apparently they were no longer worthy of the gentility of the coffee ritual.

"All right, girls . . . uh, ladies. It's all right to call you ladies, isn't it?"

"Certainly," said Charlotte crisply.

He flashed them that unnerving lips-only smile while his eyes remained cold. "You have your race."

The three women resisted the temptation to jump up and hug each other. His cold eyes told them there was a catch.

"You can have your race," he repeated, "but it will be run at the end of the racing day, after all the other races are completed, and there will be no pari-mutuel betting on it."

"No *betting?*" Charlotte was on her feet. "That's like giving us a pat on the back, then turning around and giving us a slap in the face!"

"The board decided it could not risk the potential loss of revenue. This will be a test. If the race is well attended, then next year we might repeat it with pari-mutuel betting."

"It's not likely it will be well attended if it's scheduled after the last race and nobody's got any money on the horses," said Sabina bleakly.

"You'll have press coverage," he said cheerfully.

"You bet we will," vowed Patsy.

"Well, do you want the race?" he asked.

"No," said Charlotte, "but it'll do for this year. And it's a heck of a lot better than your last offer."

Charlotte, Patsy and Sabina went to breakfast at a nearby Mexican restaurant and over huevos rancheros, they discussed their next move.

Charlotte promised to talk to the trainers and line up horses. Patsy would contact the press and Sabina would round up the jockeys. The purse money San Felipe was offering was not high enough to be an inducement. They could only hope that national publicity and the prestige of riding at San Felipe would be lure enough.

Sabina began making long-distance calls as soon as she returned home. Racetracks, for most jockeys, were transitory abodes. You went wherever you could get the best horses. Hardly any of her friends were still at the tracks where she had seen them last. A few were out with injuries. One of her favorite riders, a pioneer who had made headlines with the novelty of being a woman jock and former model ten years before, had just married a wealthy owner and had retired from racing to manage his multi-million dollar stud farm. She told Sabina she might just fly out to California in the private jet for the fun of seeing the race.

Another jockey, a thirty-year-old mother of three, was in the eighth month of her latest pregnancy. "I only ride up to the sixth month," she told Sabina. "My doctor doesn't like me to ride at all, but what the hell do male doctors know?"

Sabina smiled. Jockeys, male or female, were a breed unto themselves, the most underrated of all the daredevils, going about their daily work with a cheerful disregard for their own mortality while the Eval Knievals of the world made the headlines.

Hulking, musclebound football players, for all their macho bravado, loped into a stadium padded and armored like medieval knights while jockeys were slammed into ground every bit as hard and trampled by twelve-hundred-pound animals, protected by nothing more than a light helmet, thin silk, and two-ounce boots.

By the end of the day she had eight jockeys enthusiastically committed to the race. The women were almost as excited about getting together in one place as they were about the race itself.

While discussing the race at the dinner table that night, Miguel suggested they throw a party the night before the race in honor of the women and invite trainers, track officials and the press. "We'll do this up in style," he said. "Give the women a chance to meet people in an informal atmosphere."

Sabina did not want to argue that his home was hardly what she'd call "informal." She loved the idea of getting everyone together, but the thought of planning such a huge party was intimidating. "Miguel, I hate to tell you, but my idea of a party has always been to have people bring their own liquor while I put out potato chips, pretzels and onion dip. I don't know if I can handle something like this."

"We'll call a caterer I use," he said simply. "She'll handle all those details."

Sabina had no idea exactly how many details there were until she saw the preparations going on when she arrived home from the airport the afternoon of the party with two of the jockeys who were going to be staying at Miguel's house.

Platters of exquisite hors d'oeuvres were being prepared in the kitchen. Fresh strawberries and melon balls were in a bowl made from a watermelon carved in the shape of a basket. Roast beef, ham and turkey were being sliced. Tiny meatball creations were simmering in a large pot on the stove. The dining room table was being set buffet style with silver platters and a beautiful centerpiece of irises, daffodils and tulips.

Sabina's friends gazed about them in wonderment. Melissa Polinsky, who had helped Sabina through the tragedy of Al's death, was one of the two. She was a tiny, redhaired, freckle-faced girl with a button nose who had been nicknamed Missy, The Scarlet Bombshell, for her ability to win races and hold prodigious amounts of liquor.

"And to think I cautioned you about coming to San Felipe," she said, shaking her head. "It just goes to show you."

"Show you what?" asked dark-haired, pencil-thin Pam Rodriguez.

Missy shrugged. "Well, it ought to show you something."

At five feet, five inches, Pam towered over most jockeys, but since it was weight and not height that mattered, she had no trouble getting mounts in Illinois and Louisiana. Pam also had a deceptive way of appearing weak and vulnerable when she wanted. Sabina had seen her win a considerable fortune arm wrestling unsuspecting jockeys.

That night Sabina mused that throwing a party had never been easier—and there was not a potato chip or dish of onion dip in sight. Servants were indeed lovely—a tremendous asset, as were professional caterers.

Knowing there would be a lot of women at the party and that Miguel was something of a flirt,

Sabina decided to steel herself against the green-eyed monster. She was secure enough in his love, she told herself, not to let a little casual eye contact bother her. But to her surprise, Miguel hardly left her side. He was charming to her friends and genuinely interested in seeing that they met people and had a good time, but his attention was focused on her. They always seemed to be touching in some way. Even when they were separated across a room, they communicated with their eyes.

For a few moments they even managed to stop playing host and hostess long enough to find a small, empty couch and simply watch the spectacle of people interacting around them. It was amusing to see how couples were matching up.

"I think Patsy has finally given up on you," she whispered to him. "I hope you're not too disappointed."

"It breaks my heart, but I'll survive."

Patsy was gazing up at one of the major San Felipe trainers with rapt interest. "What do you suppose he's saying that's so fascinating?" she asked Miguel.

Miguel watched carefully, as though making an attempt to read the trainer's lips. "He is describing the finer points of thoroughbred breeding."

Frank Lathrop was coming out of the dining room with a huge plate of hors d'oeuvres and Pam Rodriguez. "Frank seems mesmerized by your friend Pam," noted Miguel.

"I thought he was more interested in the food. This is the first time I've seen him leave the dining room since he got here."

Miguel gazed at them for a moment and shook

his head. "I can't believe that woman is strong enough to do what you said."

"I'll bet you a dinner on our honeymoon that before the evening's out, Frank will have lost a pretty penny arm wrestling with her."

"The way he's looking at her, Frank's hoping for more than an arm wrestle."

"And so's poor Rich Dempsey," she added.

"He's after Pam too?"

"No. Missy. They're over by the patio door."

"Why *poor* Rich Dempsey?" asked Miguel with surprise. "He looks like he's having the time of his life over there with Missy."

"Did you notice how much booze he's consuming?"

"He is obviously planning to ply Missy with liquor, then take advantage of her," said Miguel logically.

Sabina laughed. "And Missy is thinking the same thing."

"Isn't Rich a little young for Missy?"

"She adores younger men. In fact, she once told me that latching on to a younger man is like latching on to a good colt. If you get them before they've had time to develop any bad habits, you've got yourself a prize stud later on."

Miguel chuckled. "It's not a bad theory."

"Oh," said Sabina, "they're ducking out. Going down to the bathhouse, I'll bet. That's where Missy's staying."

"It will be good for Rich." Miguel was philosophical. "We'll see if he rides any better tomorrow for it."

A reporter from one of the major Los Angeles newspapers interrupted their speculations. "Excuse me, folks, I hope I'm not interrupting things, but I just heard a tantalizing rumor over by the fireplace. Is it true that you two are engaged?"

Miguel grinned and tightened his arm around Sabina. "Don't print it until after the race tomorrow, but yes, we plan to be married the night after the San Felipe Derby."

"You're both riding in the Derby, aren't you?" They nodded.

"That doesn't bother you?"

"Does what bother us?" asked Miguel.

"Competing against each other?"

"We are looking forward to it," said Miguel. "In fact, we have our own little wager on it."

The man turned his attention on Sabina. "Wouldn't you like to see Miguel win the very last race of his career?"

"It would be a fitting end to an extraordinary career," she answered. "Sure, I'd love to see him win it."

"More than you'd like to win the Derby yourself?"

Sabina suddenly realized what he was implying. "Are you asking if I'll throw the race?"

"Not at all." He backed off. "It's just that there must be some conflict in your mind about it."

"I don't know a jockey out there who wouldn't like to see Miguel Carrasco win his last race. I love this man, and I'm making a lifetime commitment to him, but the wedding is the last thing he and I will be thinking about when the horses head into the stretch."

"On the other hand," said Miguel, "isn't it just as plausible that I would want to see Sabina win the race?"

"I suppose so." The thought didn't seem to have occurred to him.

"The San Felipe Derby is the most important race of her career. If she wins, she'll be riding Xenophon in Kentucky, maybe even to the Triple Crown."

"But what about Composure? If he wins, you'd have the same opportunity to go to Kentucky. Wouldn't you rather end your career there than in San Felipe?"

Sabina waited for his response. He seemed to be weighing the possibility, and she found herself hoping that the thought of Kentucky might make him reconsider his decision to quit racing.

"Whatever the outcome," he said after a moment, "I am ending my career at San Felipe."

Sabina was glad the party broke up early. She had to be at the track the next morning.

At first sleeping with Miguel every night had not been easy for her. The physical contact he liked during the day did not stop after they had made love. He liked to hold her through the night, sometimes caressing her in his sleep. It took her awhile not to be jarred awake by his touch. Sometimes, just falling asleep pressed up against him was difficult. Finally she discovered a place on his shoulder that seemed to have been made for her head, and by dropping her leg between his and stretching her arm across his chest, she learned to fall asleep so deeply and contentedly that he might just as well have sung her a lullaby.

Not all the caresses were in his sleep. Often she would awaken to a gentle stroking slowly arousing her passion. And they would make love in a soft, cloudy way without ever really leaving their dreams. There were mornings when she awakened wondering if they had really made love or if she had just dreamed it.

It was rare that she woke before Miguel. He was used to early-morning workouts at the track and sometimes liked to swim several laps in his pool just before dawn.

She cherished those rare occasions when she did open her eyes before he, when she could indulge herself and just gaze at the face on the pillow next to her.

It was a pleasure to see the uncharacteristic tranquility on his lively, expressive face. His sensuous lips would be slightly open, the dark eyes closed, the long lashes lying on his beard-roughened cheeks. In those unguarded moments, love for him overwhelmed her until she wanted to cry with the joy of it.

The first pale-pink light of dawn was slanting through the bedroom windows that morning as she watched him, wondering if he had been dreaming about the Derby, as she had.

She thought about what the reporter had said the night before. Deep inside she knew that she did want him to win that race. Longden had won his last race. It was the only appropriate finale for a jockey who had dedicated a lifetime to winning.

Of course there was the chance that neither one of them would have a close shot at it. You couldn't predict what was going to happen on a track. A whopping eighteen horses were entered in the Derby. Some would be taking up space only because their owners wanted the prestige of saying they had a horse in the race. But some of them were speed horses every bit as powerful as Xenophon or Composure.

Anything could happen with that many horses. She might get herself stuck on the rail and not be able to move. Composure, even though he was behaving himself lately under Miguel's constant tutoring, could suddenly regress and pull one of his old tricks.

But what if it did come down to the wire? What if she and Miguel were forced to battle it out for the lead in the last hundred yards? She had never deliberately thrown a race in her life. And in spite of the cameras, it wouldn't be that hard to do. Did she love Miguel enough to give him the most important victory of his life?

And there was something else to consider. She thought about all the races she'd run with Al. She had not wanted to face facts because she had loved him so much, but he was not the rider she was. Even when he'd had the better horse, she would finish before him. Al looked good on a horse, but he had never mastered the ability to make snap decisions in the thick of the race. The best jockeys had an almost uncanny ability to anticipate situations and take advantage of them. A few seconds often made all the difference.

Sabina had often felt guilty about those wins, and although Al never acted as though it mattered, she knew her success had eaten away at his male ego. He would take it out on her in subtle ways, staying out late with his friends, forgetting a birthday, and even on occasion flirting with other women.

There was no doubt that Miguel Carrasco was

the superior jockey, but he also had an ego. This was his last race. There would be no more races in which to regain his self-esteem. Perhaps worse than having his last race remembered as the one where he hit dirt would be having his last race remembered as the one where he was beaten by his wife.

Chapter 12

SHE GLANCED AT THE CLOCK. IF SHE DIDN'T WANT to wake him, she would have to turn off the radio alarm soon. Pulling gently away, she extricated herself from his strong encircling arm. But the movement awakened him.

He opened his eyes slowly, smiled at her and, reaching his hand up into the tangle of her long hair, pulled her head down to him. "Morning," she whispered against his lips. Her own were still numb with sleep, but he was quickly bringing them to life.

She ran the palm of her hand down his chest and abdomen, and he gave an appreciative growl of delight. Both his hands were traveling over her body, as though he had just discovered a wondrous surprise in his bed. The magic of his touch was awakening each nerve ending, making her tingle with desire for him.

"I shall never get tired of waking to find you here with me," said Miguel, his low voice still gravelly with sleep. "How I love you, Sabina *mia. Mi amor, mi vida, mi alma.*"

She loved it when he spoke Spanish; the words were like music and poetry, an essential part of Miguel.

"Oh, Miguel . . . teach me Spanish."

"I just told you that you're my love, my life, my soul. What else do you want to learn?"

His mouth was pulling on the dark areole of her breast, drawing it hard.

She moaned and laced her fingers through his thick hair. "Everything. I want to learn it all. I want to be able to talk to you in Spanish, read all the books in your library."

His fingers fanned out over her stomach and kneaded between her legs. "You are a very ambitious woman. I like that."

"And I want to know what the guys are saying when they joke around in Spanish at the track."

He laughed and, pinning her arms back, gazed into her eyes with amusement. "Now you finally admit the real reason."

"No, the real reason is that I love you so much that I don't want anything to be between us, not language, not anything."

He traced a loving finger across her lips. "Here is your first lesson. Repeat after me: *Eres mi amor, mi vida, mi alma.*"

"*Eres mi amor, mi vida, mi . . . ?*"

"*Mi alma,* my soul."

"*Mi alma.*"

"*Te quiero.* I love you."

"*Te quiero,*" she repeated.

His lips gently sealed the promise as her hand slipped down to find his hardness. "Miguel, *te quiero*."

Shifting her hips upward, she guided him into her and felt him fill her with the warmth of his love.

He thrust deeply inside her, making her tremble, then lifted her ankles, circling them around his strong neck, and drove even more profoundly into the depths of her soul.

Their eyes locked in a penetrating, unblinking gaze as they left the confines of their bodies behind. Language would never separate them, she knew. Nothing could.

They were racing now, tearing down the track in perfect rhythmic strides, gaining momentum to the pounding of heartbeats and hooves, battering the ground beneath them, propelling forward, reaching, pushing to the wire under garlands of rose petals. . . .

The harsh sound of the alarm brought them back to their own bodies, bursting the illusion, and reminding Sabina that she had to wake Pam and Missy so they could get to the track to watch workouts.

She covered Miguel's face with kisses, pulled on jeans and a T-shirt, ran downstairs and out to the back lawn toward the bathhouse. She'd wake Missy first, since she'd be the hardest to get going.

Suddenly she remembered Rich Dempsey. Was he still there? She knocked tentatively on the bedroom door instead of barging in, and was rewarded for her discretion with the sound of two groans, one male, the other female.

"Missy, do you still want to go to workouts this morning."

"Morning?" coughed Missy. "It can't possibly be morning. What happened to last night?"

There was some shuffling inside the room, and after a moment Missy appeared at the door, her red hair sticking straight out in every direction. "That kid can drink," she said with awe.

"Missy, what happened to your arm?"

Missy looked down at it, as though it were someone else's appendage. It was red and swollen around the elbow. "So that's what all the pain was."

"What on earth did you do?"

Missy scratched her head with her other hand. "We had a lot to drink. Did you know that Miguel keeps a whole stocked bar down here, too?"

"Rich didn't get rough with you, did he?" asked Sabina with alarm.

Missy giggled. "Nah. He's a cutie." She glanced over her shoulder at Rich, who was sitting up in bed, looking slightly embarrassed at being discovered there. "We went skinny-dipping sometime after midnight. We were racing each other and I got to the end of the pool, did a flip turn and miscalculated."

"Are you going to be able to ride with your arm like that?" asked Sabina.

"Oh, my God!" Missy poked at it and moaned. "Maybe it's only bruised. I hope so. Oh, hell! I come all the way out here for a chance of a lifetime ride at San Felipe and blow it before I even get on the track!"

"Don't be pessimistic. Maybe it's just bruised.

Miguel's got this orthopedic doctor. I'll have him call and make an appointment for you. You should probably have that X-rayed before you do anything."

Rich Dempsey rubbed his puffy eyes. "I'll drive Missy wherever to get that fixed," he said worriedly. "Oh, my head. I've been trampled by a dozen horses and never felt this bad before."

"Missy should have had more sense," said Pam unsympathetically as they arrived at the track a half hour later for workouts. "She's a damn good rider, but like a lot of jockeys, this wouldn't be the first race she's lost from too much partying the night before."

Pam was a disciplined athlete and vegetarian who abhored alcohol, salt and sugar with equal vehemence. She took daily vitamin supplements and consumed more carrots and oats than most of the horses she rode.

"You and Frank Lathrop seemed to be getting along well last night," said Sabina.

"He's a good-looking guy. Abominable eating habits, though. Nothing against that beautiful spread of food you and Miguel laid out, but Frank takes in entirely too much sugar. Said he was the first trainer at San Felipe to give you a mount."

"We've had some arguments. Frank likes to exercise his vocal chords, but basically he's a good guy."

"Seemed like it," agreed Pam. "That edginess is probably from the sugar. A pity, 'cause he's in pretty good shape for a man that age, and he won't stay that way for long. He asked me to gallop one of his horses this morning." She gazed around at the track, looking the palm trees up and down, surveying the elegant green art-deco building.

"Not a bad place, this San Felipe Meadows. It's freezing back in New Jersey this time of year. I never thought a woman jock would have a chance out here. You've proved us all wrong. Maybe I'll stick around for a while, see what I can scare up."

Sabina grinned. "Wish you would."

It was noon before they had word on Missy. She had chipped a bone in her arm and wouldn't be able to ride.

"What about using one of the exercise girls to fill in?" suggested Pam as several of them discussed the problem.

"I'll ride," Patsy offered quickly.

"Hold on there, Pats," said Charlotte. "You haven't been at this too long. Some of the girls have been exercising horses around here for several years, hoping to get a mount."

Patsy held her ground. "Not one of them has worked as hard as I have to get this race off the ground. I've been breaking horses from the gate, breezing them. And I've been doing a good job. I'm damn ready for a race. Ask anyone. Ask Sabina."

Sabina nodded. "She's been doing really well. I don't see any reason why she can't ride Missy's horse if the owner and trainer don't mind."

"They don't," said Patsy quickly. "I already talked to them."

Leave it to Patsy, thought Sabina with amusement. She doesn't miss an opportunity.

Patsy fell into step beside her. "Hey, thanks for speaking up for me. Listen, Sabina, I really appreciate everything you've done for me. I know a lot of the people around here think I'm pushy and don't always agree with the way I go about getting things done."

Sabina shrugged. "You get things done. That's more than a lot of people can say."

Patsy laughed. "Yeah. Guess so. For me, this is everything. I've been tossed around foster homes most of my life. My mom was an alcoholic and dumped me I don't know how many times. I don't even know where she is today. I came out here for the first time when I was sixteen and decided right then and there that this was what I wanted. It was so beautiful here, with the gardens and the sleek thoroughbreds. Well ordered, yet so . . . so exciting. I figured right then, no matter what it took, I was going to make it."

"I think you will, Patsy." Sabina gave her a hug. "Good luck this afternoon."

Patsy beamed. "Thanks; you too."

She started to head toward her car, then stopped. "Patsy . . ."

"Yeah?"

Sabina didn't really want to bring it up, but it would gnaw at her for the rest of her life if she didn't. "That morning you went to Miguel's for breakfast, did you . . ."

Patsy shook her head. "Not for lack of trying. I dropped enough hints, but he wasn't picking 'em up. I thought about it afterward. A guy like Miguel Carrasco isn't going to have any interest in me. I may have looks, but what have I accomplished in my life? Nothing, yet. That's another reason I want so badly to make it as a jockey. Someday I want to have a guy like Miguel Carrasco fall in love with me. Guys at that top rung want a woman who can hold their own with them, not just one who looks good. A winner."

Sabina felt as though a weight had been lifted off her shoulders. "Thanks, Patsy."

As Sabina had suspected, half the stands emptied out after the last race. The hardcore bettors weren't sticking around if there was no money to be won. But the press was still there and the race fans who stayed were enjoying the hoopla and novelty. The publicity had also brought out a number of people who normally wouldn't come to a racetrack.

As the women entered the jockey room, however, Sabina saw at least one advantage in leaving the all-women race until last. When she had begun riding at San Felipe, they had erected a makeshift partition in the room so she could change in privacy. But eight women were too many to change behind one small partition. For this race the women waited until all the men had cleared out, then entered the previously all-male domain.

One of the jockeys, who was in her thirties, recalled the furor that had accompanied her entrance into her first jockey room. "It was the wives who were madder than the jockeys. They didn't like the idea that I was going to see their men without much on."

"It sure is an advantage if you're going out with

any of 'em," said another of the girls with a giggle. "You know exactly what you're getting beforehand."

"I've never seen any of the guys without at least a towel," said Sabina.

"You've been racing at the wrong tracks," said Pam.

"Sabina didn't do so bad," the other said. "That Carrasco's the best-looking guy I've ever seen on or off a track. If you get tired of him, Sabina, send him to me."

"Not likely," she laughed.

The San Felipe officials had thought it appropriate to make this a race of mares and fillies, four years old and up. Sabina was riding a mare from Bardy's stable named Molly Gee.

The sight of the women parading to post gave Sabina a thrill of pride she hadn't thought she'd have. Even though she had been lukewarm about this idea to begin with, she was now glad the race had come about. They were making history at this historic race track. Even if there was no pari-mutuel betting this time, it was bound to open things up further for women.

Glancing about her, she knew that all but Patsy were experienced riders who would do a creditable job with the horses. And she had faith in Patsy, who was looking every bit the professional in her silks. She had been working hard, harder in fact than Sabina could remember of anyone. And she had come a long way in a relatively short period of time.

Pam had drawn the post position next to Sabina, and after they loaded, Pam looked over at her and said with awe, "Can you believe this, Sabina? Just look at us out here in the big time. Good feeling, eh?"

"The way it should be," said Sabina.

The latch sprang open and the horses burst forward. In those first few crucial seconds, the mare did not break well and fell behind the others.

Sabina found herself trailing last around the far turn. Patsy was just up ahead of her, inside near the rail. As Molly moved on to the bit and picked up speed, Sabina looked for a way to move up, but someone was holding down the rail and another horse was in the next lane, blocking her.

She was not dealing with the gentlemen of San Felipe Meadows. These women were used to the rough and tumble of the fair-ground circuits. They'd as soon shut her off as blink an eye.

There was nothing to do for the moment but sit tight and wait. It wasn't long before she saw her chance. A slight crack opened up as one horse drifted out. She chirped to Mollie. The mare drove through the wedge and passed several horses.

Pam, on a speed horse, had set the pace, determined to hold her position at the front all the way to the wire.

Molly Gee was striding out, but Sabina felt the animal breathing strangely and was alarmed. It was almost as though the mare were holding her breath as she accelerated, burning tremendous amounts of oxygen. Sabina turned Molly's head loose, hoping the mare would relax before she burned herself out.

It was a wise decision. Molly pulled herself together and forged ahead, coming on to Pam's mare.

Pam looked over her shoulder and used her stick for the first time. Sabina was pumping, pushing her horse. She closed to within a length and slowly, methodically, moved up until they were neck and neck.

They were in the closing yards. Sabina went to her stick again and Molly Gee strode out. Pam's horse, who had kept a fast pace throughout the race, was tiring, and despite Pam's urging, began to fall back.

In the last two hundred yards, Molly Gee rushed forward to win by three lengths.

Patsy had finished sixth in a field of eight, but she was still elated. It had been, after all, her first race, and she hadn't done anything to disgrace herself. "Wow, that was even more fun than I thought it would be!" she said to Sabina as they pulled up and turned the horses around.

All eight women, arms draped around each other, posed for pictures on the track and chatted with reporters for the TV cameras.

Miguel was waiting for Sabina at the tunnel. He threw his arms around her, lifting her off the ground as he kissed her.

In the next minute the TV cameras were focused on them and reporters, sensing another story, began plying them with questions.

It was the beginning of a media furor, Sabina learned, that would not let up until the day of the Derby.

Chapter 13

THE NEWS MEDIA SEEMED INSATIABLE IN ITS CURIOS-
ity. There were no royal weddings in Britain, no
major scandals breaking in Washington, D.C., no
surprise *coup d'états* or natural disasters to rivet
the public's attention.

"There is always a great deal written about the
San Felipe Derby," Miguel told her, "because it's
the prelude to Kentucky. People all around the
world are watching. Usually the writers who know
nothing about horses are at a loss for things to
say. Sabina, think how happy we must be making
those editors by giving them some romance to
write about. We're both on favored horses. We're
in love. You cannot blame the media for exploit-
ing it."

"Yes I can," said Sabina angrily. "Every day
they're out at the track swooping down on us like
vultures, and then lurking outside the house. I

can't take a step out at the track without somebody shoving a microphone under my nose or
snapping my picture. I wouldn't mind talking
about Xenophon or the race or even the plight of
women jockeys. But it's such an intrusion of
privacy for them to ask me about you. Our
personal feelings are none of their damn business!"

"Don't let it bother you," said Miguel in that
calming tone that had made a gentleman out of
Composure.

"Bother me? Look at this." She thrust a su-
permarket tabloid at him. The bold headline
read:

TENDER IS THE TURF
Will Love or Greed Decide the Derby?

"They're calling our integrity into question.
. . . Isn't that libelous or slanderous or something?" she argued.

"Forget it," he said, dropping the newspaper
into the trash.

"And what about this one?" she handed him
another.

Splashed on the page was a photo that had been
taken just after her win on Marshall George. She
was covered head to toe with mud, looking like a
drowned rat in the pouring rain. Juxtaposed was a
photo of Miguel, suave and debonair in a tuxedo,
a glamorous Natasha in a sparkling beaded gown
on his arm. There was another photo of him
sunning on a yacht with a pretty socialite on the
French Riviera.

The headline was:

MUD IN HIS EYE?

"Some psychic is claiming I bewitched you!"

"That's true." He gave her a kiss on the cheek.

"And she's also saying that while you're under my spell I'm going to make you throw the race. A pop psychologist is backing her up, saying that on your last fall from Composure you knocked a screw loose and you're completely under my power."

Miguel laughed.

"These things don't bother you?" she asked incredulously.

"I don't think anyone takes them seriously."

"Well, look at this."

In bold letters across the page were the words:

PHOTO FETISH AT SAN FELIPE?

"They claim that they talked to several of your friends and Natasha. The night I went to visit you after you got out of the hospital, they say that I was in bed making love with you while the other jockeys stood around having a party and taking pictures of us."

A dark, murderous look came into his eyes as he took the newspaper and read the article. Without putting it down he picked up the phone and called his lawyer.

Sabina didn't know whether or not it was due to the phone call, but the tone of the articles began to change. The headline the next day made the romance into a frothy Cinderella–Prince Charming saga:

HEARTS AND FLOWERS AND ALFALFA

The photo they used this time had been snapped as Miguel had lifted her off the ground in a hug after she'd won her last race.

Two groups of people were ecstatic over the coverage: the San Felipe press department and the jockeys.

Bob Perile announced that the excitement over Miguel and Sabina had boosted attendance at the track by twenty-five percent.

And overnight the numbers of mini-skirted jockey chasers swelled. For the first time in their lives jockeys were being portrayed as the handsome, swashbuckling romantic heroes they had always known they were. After every race they were besieged by autograph and romance seekers.

Sabina was still exercising horses in the mornings and riding from two to three races an afternoon. There had been another win, a second and a third, and she had fought hard for every one.

For the most part she was still riding longshots. It was only to be expected of the relatively "new kid on the block," but the prejudice against her as a woman seemed to have disappeared. Those trainers who had thought her an exception to the rule had been surprised at the quality of riding they'd seen in the all-women race.

After the thrill of riding in her first race Patsy left San Felipe for Arizona, where it would be easier to get mounts.

Pam had an offer from a northern California trainer who'd seen her ride that day and had been impressed. Since the San Felipe meet was almost over, she thought she'd go to the San Francisco Bay area for a while and return to Southern California for the racing season in San Diego.

Three days before the Derby Bardy asked Sabina to take Xenophon for a "sharpener," a three-eighths mile sprint workout.

That kind of strenuous training didn't work for all horses, but Xenophon seemed to thrive on hard work, the faster the better.

Sabina arrived at the barn just as the groom was putting the saddle on his back. "This is one big horse," he said as he tightened the girth around him. "Seems like every time I saddle him I need a bigger cinch."

He was sixteen hands, two inches and 1,159 pounds. Sportswriters were comparing him to Man O' War and Secretariat.

She watched with awe as the groom led him out into the area between the barns where she would mount. Sabina couldn't remember seeing a fitter horse. The sinewy muscles rippled as sunlight dappled his shiny brown coat. The horse playfully kicked out his heels and nipped at the groom.

"He's feeling good," said the groom.

"So am I," said Sabina.

Bardy and Xenophon's owner walked behind her and the pony rider, heading toward the grandstands with their clockwatches. She could tell by the look in their eyes that they thought they had a winner.

As she reached the gap that led onto the main track Xenophon stopped and watched the other horses for a moment. His ears pricked up and his neck stiffened as he saw Miguel on Composure flying around the turn, also on a "sharpener."

"That's the horse they say might beat you," she told Xenophon as she urged him out onto the track.

He grunted and did a few dance steps to the side. "That's what I thought you'd say," she chuckled.

A few minutes later she saw Miguel heading back at a walk after his workout.

"How'd he do?" she asked him.

"Sensational."

"Xenophon just told me you don't have a chance against him."

"We'll see about that, Xenophon," he said with a laugh.

The night before the race they swam a mile in the pool, had a light dinner and went upstairs to soak in the Jacuzzi.

"I can't believe it's finally here," she said dreamily as she floated to the surface with the bubbles.

"The wedding or the race?" he asked with amusement.

"Both." She laughed, then grew serious. "Miguel, I think I'm going to ride the winner. I really do."

"That should make you happy, *mi amor.*" He reached out and settled her on his lap. Pushing her long hair away, he kissed her neck.

"I know it should make me happy, but if you want to know the truth, I keep thinking about what all those reporters were saying."

"Don't be silly. When you are out there, you are not going to be thinking of anything but winning that race."

"But you don't understand, Miguel. . . . It's deeper than that. I guess it's left over from Al. Whenever we rode against each other, I had the same queasy feeling. Nine times out of ten, unless I was on a horse headed for the glue factory, I beat him. He was always good-natured about it, and congratulated me, but the resentment would come out. He'd stay out late drinking with the guys, or he'd forget my birthday or he'd flirt with another woman at a party. And there were those times, too, that he . . .'"

Miguel wrapped his powerful arms around her. "It's not going to be like that with us tomorrow."

"How do you know, Miguel? You've never been beat out there by a woman, much less the woman you're going to marry. You think you're liberated, but you have all that Latin conditioning about a woman's place. How do you know how you'll react?"

"I know," he said simply, "because Composure is going to win the race."

"You're that sure?"

"The horse is in peak condition."

She ran a hand over the taut muscles of his shoulders and arms. Then she thought of Xenophon. Both superb animals. "So are you. It seems strange to think of you retiring. Are you sure you want to do it?"

He hesitated for a moment. "I think it's time."

"But you love the sport so, and you're in better shape than a lot of sixteen-year-olds. Thirty-eight isn't like one foot in the grave. Longden raced

until he was fifty-nine. Willie Shoemaker, one of
the finest athletes who ever lived, is over fifty and
still winning."

"Shoemaker and Longden are extraordinary,
unusual examples. You know that, Sabina. Most
jockeys have retired by my age."

"You're every bit as extraordinary and unusual!"

He kissed her lightly on the lips. "Your motiva-
tions are suspect. I think you want me to reconsider because if I decide to stay in racing, I won't
feel so much pressure to go out there and beat the
boots off you tomorrow."

"Believe it or not, I just want you to be happy.
And you're right—my motives are selfish. I'm
planning to spend the rest of my life with you, and
if you're miserable and cranky and bored because
you're not racing, it's not going to be very pleasant for me or our half-dozen little jockeys in
training."

He lifted her off his lap and got out of the
Jacuzzi, going to fetch their thick terry-cloth
robes, which had been warming near the heater.

She watched him from the back, the water
dripping off his skin, the muscles bulging beneath
it. He might have been a model for a classical
Greek statue. She had never seen a man's body
that was as beautifully put together. He had
conditioned and molded it that way for one
reason, to win horse races. And after tomorrow
that would be all over.

He helped her out of the Jacuzzi and wrapped
her snuggly in the long, warm robe. There was a
blazing fire in the fireplace in the bedroom. The

maid had put on the pale-blue satin sheets and turned the bed down for them.

Miguel went to the bar and poured them both a small snifter of cognac. "I think we should toast our last night together as an unmarried couple," he said as he handed her the glass.

"Here's to lots of little Carrascos in racing silks," she said, raising her glass.

"And here's to the Derby," he replied with a grin.

Chapter 14

THEY SIPPED THEIR COGNAC AND LOOKED AT EACH other quietly, thinking about the future.

She thought again about her life with Al. Coming to California after his death had been more than a way to escape the painful memories of the Midwest, she finally admitted. For years she had been ready to tackle the high-powered racetracks of California or New York. Out of love for Al and consideration for his ego, she had held back her own career.

Miguel's ego was not nearly as fragile. He was at the top of his profession. He had always associated with women who were extraordinary achievers. Patsy had been right about that. Even the society girl who lounged so decoratively on the Côte d'Azur yacht ran a multi-million dollar high fashion house in Paris.

For Miguel, the ultimate turn-on had been to

find a woman who was at the top of his own difficult and dangerous profession. But could he take being beaten by her at what he did best?

"I was just thinking," she murmured as he took her in his arms.

"About the race?" He was raining light kisses on her forehead.

"Sort of."

"I have you in a very compromising position, *amigita*. Are you going to reveal your strategy for tomorrow?"

She smiled and squirmed under him, feeling the texture of his coarse chest hair against her breasts. "That would not be playing fair."

"Then what were you thinking?" His hands swept magically over her body. It *was* a compromising position.

"I was just thinking how much fun it would be to keep racing against you. I mean, if nothing else, it would keep us on our toes."

He chuckled. "You really don't want me to quit, do you?"

"Miguel, I want you to do what will make you happy."

"This makes me happy." His hand slid down over her belly and thrust between her legs.

"Me, too," she whispered.

The strong fingers, so sensitive to the subtle changes of a horse's mouth, stroked and probed with uncanny, almost magical awareness of her needs, sending her soaring.

She knew she had the same mystical power over him and let her fingers glide and rub. The sounds of his feral groans echoed her own lightning passion.

Her tongue lingered in the crook of his arm. He tasted and smelled delicious. She wanted to taste all of him, all the wonderful hills and valleys of his magnificent body. She wanted to give him pleasure that he'd never known before, to fill him with the love he had given her.

"Miguel . . . Miguel . . ." His name burst from her lips, sounding like an animal cry in the night.

Her fingernails bit into his strong shoulders as they joined together. Falling back helplessly against the satin pillows, she strained against him, the waves flowing around her, pulsing like heartbeats.

And suddenly the huge bed hardly seemed large enough to contain them as the breathless turbulence of their love flung them like a hurricane. He was like a shaft of lightning inside her, making her glow and burn with swirling flames.

Crashing and exploding into a passionate flurry of tremors, they held each other, licked the moisture from each other's skin, and with silent understanding began again.

Sunday morning was a workday like any other at the track. There were stalls to muck out, water buckets to clean, hooves to be picked and brushed with mineral oil, horses to exercise and hot-walk.

It was more like summer than it had been in a long time. By eight o'clock the exercise riders already had their jackets off.

It seemed to Sabina that there was a different feeling in the air that morning. The trainers who had horses entered in the Derby all wore taut, street-map lined faces and spoke in low voices to the owners and jockeys.

With eighteen entrants, the gross purse was $548,350. The winning horse would receive $323,350; second, $100,000; third, $75,000; fourth $37,500 and fifth, $12,500. The winning jockeys would take the standard ten percent.

Sabina stopped to take a look at Xenophon. He was standing at the back of his stall. He didn't come out to greet her.

"He's just thinking about the race," said the groom when he saw her worried expression. "Gets kind of sulky-like sometimes before a big one. Bardy had me turn him out for a few minutes in the sun pen early this morning, and he was full of it. Kicking up his heels like he was ready to do the polka."

"Polka! Wash your mouth out. He's going to do the Charleston this afternoon if I have anything to say about it."

By ten o'clock the parking lots were filling up and access roads to the track were so clogged that it was being estimated they would have a record crowd of over seventy thousand. Most of them, surmised Sabina, were news people. Everywhere she turned there seemed to be a camera facing her. It was like being trapped in a hall of mirrors.

After workouts she ducked away from the reporters and went home to have a light brunch with Miguel. He had already done a leisurely four miles in the pool and was in top spirits.

She did a few laps just to relax, changed, and then they drove to the track together.

Cameras were set up, waiting to catch them in the parking area outside the jockey room.

"Are you nervous about the race?"

"I've been around too long to get nervous," answered Miguel.

"You think you have the winning horse?"

"I have a damn good horse."

"You don't think he'll pull something freaky on you like he did the last time you rode him?"

"I hope not."

"What about you, Miss Martin? Are you nervous?"

"No. I'm too busy figuring out how I'm going to win."

"And how will that be?"

She smiled. "I never give away my strategy before a race."

"Have you discussed it with Miguel?"

They glanced at each other and grinned, remembering the delightfully compromising position they had found themselves in the night before.

"We're still discussing marriage strategy," said Miguel.

"Who's going to be the boss?"

"We're going to alternate," joked Sabina. "He'll be boss one week and I'll take over the next."

"Where do you plan to honeymoon?"

"Kentucky," they both said together, then laughed. The response hadn't been planned.

Extricating themselves from the reporters, they made their way to the jockey's room. She was riding one of Frank's horses in the first race. Miguel went up to the Turf Club to watch.

Cameras were turned on her again as she walked down the stairs from the jockey's room into the saddling area. She tried to stop feeling self-conscious and to concentrate on the race.

It was a six-furlong claiming race for four-year-olds and up. She was on a five-year-old gelding who had not won a race in months. He was a 40-1 shot.

"Just do what you can," said Frank as he gave her a leg up.

Sabina had never seen so many people crowded into the paddock area. They were standing up on benches, hanging from trees. She heard the murmurs as she rode by.

"She's just a little bit of a thing."

"Do you really think she cast a spell on him?"

"She's prettier than her pictures."

"Have you seen *him?* He's gorgeous. Those eyes!"

A woman called out loudly in a raucous whiskey voice, "Go get 'em, lady jock!"

The giggling, gum-chewing jockey chasers were out in force, lined up at the tunnel. Since it was a hot day, many were in skimpy halters and shorts, young breasts bursting over the tops, and bottoms hanging provocatively out. The jockeys pretended to ignore them as they rode by.

She looked up briefly and saw Miguel on the balcony. He waved to her, then slipped back up the ramp away from the crowd.

As she had expected, the gelding tired quickly, perspiring and breathing badly in the heat. She had a difficult time getting him to move on to the bit and had almost given up when he seemed to perk up with a slight burst of energy down the stretch. But it was too late. She finished tenth in a field of eleven.

As she walked back through the tunnel with Frank, somebody yelled, "Ya oughta stay home and cook for Carrasco."

"I can't cook, either," she sniped back.

It was not an auspicious beginning for her racing day.

Miguel joined her. "You didn't tell me you couldn't cook." He gave her an accusing look. "The wedding is off. We'll starve to death."

"I am not totally without talents," she shot back with a grin. "I'm a whiz with a can of tuna."

"In that case we can get married. What a relief."

With horror she suddenly realized that their whole exchange had been recorded by a television crew. Unable to contain himself any longer, the reporter snidely asked Miguel what he thought of his fiancée's last race.

Frank answered for him. And for once Sabina was grateful for his volatile temper. "Jesus, give it a rest, you flaky bastards!"

Some children pushed their way through the camera crews. "Sabina, Miguel, can we have your autographs?"

Back inside the haven of the jockey's room, she leaned up against the cool wall and sighed. "It's a madhouse out there."

Miguel was glancing around the familiar surroundings. It had been awhile since he had seen it, and Sabina sensed he was feeling good about being back.

He joked with his friends, watching the previous races on videotape, discussing the way the fields had shaped up. She had forgotten what an integral part of that group he was. When she had first arrived at San Felipe she had taken his magnetic presence there for granted. But now she could see the difference he made. He was a catalyst. Conversations became livlier when he was in the room and the jokes flew faster.

Several of his friends said out loud what she was feeling, what they all had to be feeling: it was too soon for Miguel Carrasco to quit. He had too many good years left.

Just before they were called into the saddling area, Miguel gave her a hug. They kissed lightly, smiled and wished each other luck.

The cameras were pinned on them as they descended the stairs, but this time Sabina could legitimately ignore them. She was thinking only of Xenophon and the race.

He was dancing around in the saddling area looking cocky and anxious to go. The groom gave her a wink. "You're right. I think it's going to be the Charleston."

Bardy checked the horse out head to toe, then accompanied Sabina to the walking ring. "With all those horses there's bound to be a traffic jam, so see if you can place him in front at the start. But if you can't, keep him out of trouble. Circle wide around if you have to, but not so wide you end up out in the parking lot or something. You know the horse. Just use your own judgment."

"Riders up," called the paddock judge.

Bardy grabbed her boot and boosted her onto the horse. As she tied the knot in the reins he said, "Don't forget to warm him up. I know it's hot out, but he's a little muscle tight."

She nodded. It was late afternoon. A slight breeze had come up and was blowing the horses' manes and tails, billowing out the colorful jockey silks.

Miguel looked confident and relaxed as they came through the tunnel and out into the golden afternoon sunlight, enjoying every minute of his last race.

The crowds went crazy when they saw him. People were standing up, waving their arms, shouting his name. Filled beyond capacity, the grandstands and infield were a sea of sparkling bright colors and faces. This was the race they had all come to see.

Xenophon stopped for a moment, pricked up his ears and gazed around, seeming to be in awe of the huge, moving, vocal mass of humanity.

A brass band started up, and he danced sideways in time to the music. Composure, hearing the music, laid his ears back and kicked out at the pony rider. Sabina held her breath. Was he back to his old tricks?

A streak of fear washed down her back. Suddenly she didn't want Miguel back in racing again. He was always riding the outlaws nobody else could handle. Maybe Dr. Backer was right. Miguel was bound to have more accidents if he continued racing. She hated herself for having suggested he continue. For the moment she stopped seeing things as a jockey. The wife in her wanted him safe from harm.

As they headed toward the upper stretch on the way to the gate, she turned to Bonnie, who was on the pony accompanying them. "Just go alongside me. I'm going to warm him up a bit."

Some of the eighteen horses were already "washy" from the heat. She checked Xenophon's shoulders for signs that he was nervous or warm. The veins were not bulging, nor did he feel hot to the touch.

Gathering up the reins, she sent Xenophon into a slow gallop around the turn. When he began to feel smooth and limber, she eased the colt up and turned around.

There were so many horses that an auxiliary gate had been set up to accommodate them all. Sabina had never ridden in as large a race. With so many horses breaking from the gate at once, it could be dangerous.

There had been a great deal of discussion before the race about the advantages and disadvantages of the post positions in such a large field. Most experts felt that horses breaking from outside posts would have the hardest time, for they would have to move into the track when it narrowed.

"It'll be like a funnel out there at the sixteenth pole," Paul had said before the race. The traffic jam that Bardy had predicted. One of the trainers even threatened to withdraw his horse if he drew an outside post.

Bardy had been disappointed when Xenophon drew post fifteen. "Well, at least you'll have the length of the stretch to get placed," he told her. "I'd rather have you out there where you have room to maneuver rather than bunched up and stuck in the middle when that track narrows."

Miguel was even further out, in post position eighteen. They gazed at each other through their goggles, smiled, but said nothing.

She grabbed the lock of mane and readied herself.

The latch sprang. Xenophon was having a difficult time, floundering in his struggle to leave the gate. Staying calm, she steadied herself and waited for him to settle into his stride.

In the meantime, the other horses took off around him. She could see the green-and-white of Miguel's silks far up ahead. He wasn't wasting any time finding a good position. With Composure's speed and stamina, all he had to do was get out in front and stay there to win the race.

Slowly Xenophon was finding his footing, leveling out. Sabina knew the colt needed time to gather himself together, and didn't rush him.

Into the first turn she had the first signs that he was developing his usual rhythm, picking up momentum. Relaxed, he was running effortlessly. It was then that Sabina knew she had a chance.

Taking Bardy's advice, she kept out of trouble on the outside of the field, even though circling around all those horses meant losing some ground.

She was beginning to feel the lowering of the colt's mass as he stretched out. There was a lot of horse under her.

Miguel had Composure laying second on the rail. He was riding brilliantly, forcing the pace so that the lead horse was tiring. It could be the finest race of his life. He had Composure in excellent shape, the horse was gliding gracefully, the hooves barely seeming to touch the ground.

After swinging widely around the pack, she sensed that Xenophon was ready. She let him out, and he drove like lightning to the lead.

Miguel was now first, two lengths ahead of the

rest. As she came up on him, he glanced over at her. He was grinning. It was like that day in the park. He was having the time of his life.

"Where've you been?" he called over to her.

"Just hanging around on the backstretch, waiting to come get you."

"Like hell you will!"

She saw him uncock his stick, and in that split second, she flashed her own in front of Xenophon's right eye and began to pass Composure.

Sabina threw all her weight and strength into building Xenophon's momentum, using the rhythm to push him ahead. But she was still only a half length ahead.

This was what the seventy thousand people had come to see. The mass of bodies rose, arms waving. The rumble of their voices grew to a deafening roar as the two horses battled their way into the stretch.

Miguel didn't let her keep the lead for long. He was riding hard. "What a race, eh, *mi amor?*" he called to her as Composure pulled slightly ahead.

They rode furiously, alternately pumping and going to the stick, switching from right to left.

She could feel the beginnings of fatigue, but Xenophon was not wavering, and neither was Composure. They raced as a team neck and neck into the last hundred yards.

The roar from the crowds swelled up around them forming a wall of sound so solid she could no longer hear the hooves pounding the ground under them.

She knew they were yelling for Miguel to win. Damn, but he deserved it, the last race of his life.

She could ease up slightly and no one would know. They would think that Xenophon had legitimately tired.

But even as the thought crossed her mind, she knew she couldn't throw the race. She loved him, but if he wanted that last win, he'd have to pull it off by himself. She had never purposely thrown a race, and she wasn't going to start now.

In the next second they were under the wire together.

An eerie stillness descended on the crowds as the photo sign went up on the tote board. Moments went by. She and Miguel pulled their horses up and walked them back to the winners' circle at a leisurely pace. It was like the aftermath of making love, all feeling and not much to say. He was smiling at her, his dark eyes sparkling. How she hated to see him leave racing. It was out here that he was the most alive.

As much as she had wanted to win in those last blazing seconds, she now wanted the victory again for Miguel.

Her emotions were tumbling around inside her as they waited for the results of the photos. The number came up. Fifteen.

It took a second for the number to register on Sabina. She saw Miguel grin at her and blow her a kiss. "Go get it, pretty one!"

The grandstands erupted again.

Numbly she went through the routine of the winners' circle, managing to smile as the cameras snapped. She was holding a dozen roses. Bardy and Xenophon's owner were congratulating her, kissing her on each cheek.

She looked around for Miguel, anxious to be

with him. There was that queasy feeling in the pit of her stomach. Would it be like Al? Would he find some subtle way to get back at her?

How much easier it would have been not to have won. Oh, my God, she thought to herself. This is crazy! I've just won the race of my life. I'm on my way to Kentucky, and I'm hating myself for having done it!

Miguel was waiting for her at the tunnel. She felt his strong arms go around her, pulling her tight, felt his lips on hers.

Everything was all right. She knew that now and gave herself up to the love that enveloped them. This wasn't Al. There would be no revenge.

"You were brilliant," he said enthusiastically. "The way you anticipated my going to the stick. Sabina, you're going to give me a run in Kentucky."

"Kentucky?" she asked him, bewildered.

"They want to race Composure. And why not? It was damn close this afternoon."

The excitement bubbled up inside her. "You're going to ride Composure in Kentucky?"

He hugged her tighter. "Somebody's got to give you a little trouble. There wasn't a soul out there today who could catch you."

They headed back through the tunnel arm and arm. "Oh, darling, and after Kentucky?" She didn't dare hope.

He kissed her on the tip of her nose. "This was one hell of a good time, this afternoon. Didn't you think so?"

"The best," she agreed.

"That's what I kept thinking as we were flying

under the wire. Do you realize how fortunate we are to be able to do this for a living? I can't give it up. Not yet. I figure I'll stick around the track at least a few more years. If for nothing else, to keep you on your toes."

She threw herself into his arms and felt the warm wonderful rumble of his laughter vibrate through her.

As Miguel had said, it was going to be one hell of a good time.

Genuine Silhouette sterling silver bookmark for only $15.95!

What a beautiful way to hold your place in your current romance! This genuine sterling silver bookmark, with the distinctive Silhouette symbol in elegant black, measures 1½" long and 1" wide. It makes a beautiful gift for yourself, and for every romantic you know! And, at only $15.95 each, including all postage and handling charges, you'll want to order several now, while supplies last.

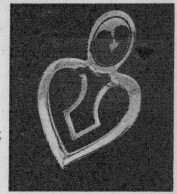

Send your name and address with check or money order for $15.95 per bookmark ordered to

Simon & Schuster Enterprises
120 Brighton Rd., P.O. Box 5020
Clifton, N.J. 07012
Attn: Bookmark

Bookmarks can be ordered pre-paid only. No charges will be accepted. Please allow 4-6 weeks for delivery.

N.Y. State Residents
Please Add Sales Tax

Silhouette Intimate Moments

more romance, more excitement

———————— **$2.25 each** ————————

Silhouette Intimate Moments

more romance, more excitement

#25 ☐ THIS MAGIC MOMENT
Nora Roberts

#26 ☐ OLD LOVE, NEW LOVE
Jane Clare

#27 ☐ DIANA'S FOLLY
Jillian Blake

#28 ☐ WALTZ IN SCARLET
Muriel Bradley

#29 ☐ A SECRET SPLENDOR
Erin St. Claire

#30 ☐ RACE AGAINST THE WIND
Sue Ellen Cole

#31 ☐ STAR SPANGLED DAYS
Jennifer West

#32 ☐ DANGEROUS PARADISE
Joanna Kenyon

**LOOK FOR INTERESTED PARTIES
BY BROOKE HASTINGS
AVAILABLE IN FEBRUARY AND
WIDOW WOMAN BY PARRIS AFTON BONDS
IN MARCH.**

Silhouette Intimate Moments

Coming Next Month

Endings And Beginnings by Nora Roberts

Liv Carmichael, Washington anchorwoman, always wanted to be the first to get the story. T.C. Thorpe was her business rival. But professional rivalry was forgotten the day T.C. became a madman's pawn and Liv's heart was held hostage with him.

Lover In The Rough by Elizabeth Lowell

Reba Farrall, connoisseur of jewels, and Chance Walker who searched the world for gems, met in Death Valley— and there they found life. Reba was a treasure beyond price, but the precious tourmaline that tied them together also drove them apart.

Moments Harsh, Moments Gentle by Joan Hohl

Amidst the glamour and flash of Atlantic City's casino row, Nacia Barns decided if ever there was a man worth risking her heart for, it was Jared Ranklin. And with a throw of the dice, Nacia staked her heart—and her future.

Designs by Lynda Trent

Shannon DuVall had been born to wealth and brought up in a home where money and position were all. Josh Calger was a cowboy who had struck it rich, a diamond in the rough—a man her family would never approve.